GWASANAETH LLYFRGELL WRECSAM
WREXHAM LIBRARY SERVICE

Withdrawn
from stock

Tynnwyd
o stoc

5/25

SPECIAL MESSAGE TO READERS
This book is published under the auspices of
THE ULVERSCROFT FOUNDATION
(registered charity No. 264873 UK)
Established in 1972 to provide funds for
research, diagnosis and treatment of eye diseases.
Examples of contributions made are: —
A Children's Assessment Unit at
Moorfield's Hospital, London.

•

Twin operating theatres at the
Western Ophthalmic Hospital, London.

•

A Chair of Ophthalmology at the
Royal Australian College of Ophthalmologists.

•

The Ulverscroft Children's Eye Unit at the
Great Ormond Street Hospital For Sick Children,
London.

You can help further the work of the Foundation
by making a donation or leaving a legacy. Every
contribution, no matter how small, is received
with gratitude. Please write for details to:
THE ULVERSCROFT FOUNDATION,
The Green, Bradgate Road, Anstey,
Leicester LE7 7FU, England.
Telephone: (0116) 236 4325

In Australia write to:
THE ULVERSCROFT FOUNDATION,
c/o The Royal Australian and New Zealand
College of Ophthalmologists,
94-98, Chalmers Street, Surry Hills,
N.S.W. 2010, Australia

THE LONELY ASTRONOMER

The great Metropolitan Observatory was the pride of 22nd century engineering and science. When the astronomer Dr. Henry Brunner was found there, battered and strangled to death, there were four suspects with reasons to hate him: his immediate assistants, and the janitor who owned a fantastic Martian spider pet ... Scientific detective Adam Quirke was called in to investigate the seemingly insoluble mystery. What was the connection between the star Betelgeuse, which Brunner had been studying, and the astronomer's murder?

JOHN RUSSELL FEARN

THE LONELY
ASTRONOMER

WREXHAM C.B.C. LIBRARY
LLYFRGELL B.S. WRECSAM

2054

ULV
A-FIC   £8.99

Complete and Unabridged

LINFORD
Leicester

First published in Great Britain

First Linford Edition
published 2007

Copyright © 1953 by John Russell Fearn
Copyright © 2006 by Philip Harbottle
All rights reserved

British Library CIP Data

Fearn, John Russell, *1908 – 1960*
    The lonely astronomer.—Large print ed.—
Linford mystery library
    1. Murder—Investigation—Fiction
    2. Astronomical observatories—Fiction
    3. Detective and mystery stories
    4. Large type books
    I. Title
    823.9'12 [F]

ISBN 978–1–84617–834–4

Published by
F. A. Thorpe (Publishing)
Anstey, Leicestershire

Set by Words & Graphics Ltd.
Anstey, Leicestershire
Printed and bound in Great Britain by
T. J. International Ltd., Padstow, Cornwall

This book is printed on acid-free paper

1

Dr. Brunner Makes Enemies

The Metropolitan Observatory was Man's answer to the problem of erecting an observatory at a height of two miles and making sure it remained steady. No mountain had proven suitable within the British aegis, due to the tendency to cloud formation. Yet an Observatory had been erected, using equally balanced magnets at ground level, which directed their attraction on the amazing creation from four sides simultaneously.

The site occupied by the Metropolitan Observatory was over five square miles in area, a park-like space broken only by the relatively small administrative buildings. In the centre of the park was the base of the mighty 'Column' upon the top of which the Observatory was poised. It had been built in 2190, and in 2191, after a year of stresses and strains, for even yet the weather was not entirely subjugated, the Observatory still stood impregnably, perched above the clouds as a rule, except during heavy weather. The supporting pillar was so designed that it expanded and contracted in the centre under wind-force, much after the principle of a centrifugal governor.

The Metropolitan Observatory was indeed the pride of British engineers. It contained instruments that challenged the best in the world, even the superlative equipment of Mount Palomar. True, the air at the top of the Column was somewhat attenuated, but it occasioned nothing more than a slight shortness of breath. The main thing was that human beings could live in comparative comfort in this astronomical 'crow's nest' and produce results that compared favourably with, and very often superseded, those of the world's more conveniently placed observatories.

In spite of this isolation high in the sky, the staff did not remain cut off from the world. A fast elevator operated within the central Column, transferring them from top to bottom — or vice versa — within a matter of minutes . . . Londoners were used to this mighty Column rearing like a metallic beanstalk until it made one dizzy to study it. Indeed, people on the south coast and in the Midlands, could see the Column's top on a fine day.

Then in April, 2191, something happened which brought the Metropolitan Observatory even more into the public eye than usual, and the business began on a quiet routine evening on April 7. On this date, as on any other, the usual staff was congregated in the Observatory for the normal spell of duty. By day, unless solar observations were called for, most of the work was done in the administrative buildings below.

The staff comprised Dr. Henry Brunner, the taciturn fifty-year-old chief, descended from a German family and still having much of the Teuton in his make-up; Monica Adley, twenty-five-year-old assistant spectrographist; David Calhoun, thirty-year-old assistant astronomer; and Joe. Nobody knew Joe's surname except the Executive. He was the janitor, preparer-of-meals, caretaker, and general factotum. There was also one other, with whom the Earth people associated only when duty demanded. This 'other' was Sasmo of the 27th Generation, a being who claimed his antecedents came from a planet circling the star Procyon. They had come to Earth in their wanderings, and in the journey twenty-seven generations had come and gone before the end of the awful voyage across the endless endlessness of space.

For the first ten years after his arrival on Earth, Sasmo had been a virtual prisoner of the scientific establishment, and subjected to numerous tests to see if he had brought any dangerous bacteria or diseases with him. The tests proved negative. He had learned to speak English within a relatively short time, and was then subjected to endless questioning from scientists, some of which was televised to a curious public. Eventually the novelty of his arrival waned and, after ten years, following pressure from various libertarian groups, he had been allowed to pass freely into society, and to make his own living.

The Observatory Executive had appointed Sasmo because he was a brilliant astronomical worker and his foreknowledge of much of the Procyon system had done much to further scientific data in this direction. Otherwise he was an 'outsider' and even more of an alien than those people who had been born and bred on Mars, a planet which had been successfully colonized ... Apparently Sasmo had been the only survivor of his voyaging race. Certainly no other like him had ever been seen on Earth.

This group, with the exception of the janitor who had his own quarters below the observatory proper, gathered as usual on the evening of April 7 to commence routine work. Dr. Brunner, as head of the proceedings, briefly looked over each member of his staff and then spoke in his thick Teutonic voice.

'I have received instructions from the Executive that we are to complete our observations of Neptune and Pluto and then assess the possibilities of extreme outer space. Since each planet is now well within range of our Earth spaceships, it obviously becomes necessary for us to discover what lies beyond our immediate system, and chart the course as far ahead as possible. Understood?'

The others nodded but said nothing.

'Tonight our final observations regarding Neptune and Pluto must be completed and then submitted to the Executive. For myself, I intend to work an extra night-long session in order to complete certain data I have worked on concerning Betelgeuse. None of you will be needed for that, so when your present work is completed you are at liberty to leave in the normal way . . . '

Brunner paused, but he did not add the usual word of dismissal. Instead his attention was fixed on something in a far corner of the observatory. At length he compressed his thick lips and turned sharply to the bell-push which connected with the janitor's quarters below. Nobody said anything, but Monica Adley and David Calhoun glanced towards the corner that had attracted the doctor's attention — then they started very slightly and watched in fascinated interest the swift, unerring activity of Loony, the Martian gossamer-spider.

Gossamer-spiders from Mars were by no means rare on Earth. They had been created by the scientists on Mars over a period of years — mutations engendered in a specially cultivated forest environment under colossal pressurised domes. In appearance they were similar to the Earth-spider, but of far greater size. Further, they were extremely intelligent, and spent their time when not sleeping spinning the most intricately woven webs. These webs were always tightly knitted so as to form an almost complete web 'fabric' — yet they were transparent to light and glittered and flowed like phantasmal rainbows. Yes, the gossamer-spider was quite the most intriguing pet ever known — but the sternly scientific observatory was no place for the labours of this particular one.

'Yes, doctor?' Joe came into view through the trapdoor from below. He was nearly sixty, very myopic, and invariably clad in dusty-looking coveralls.

'*That* is yours, I think?' Brunner looked coldly towards the rainbow-hued insect busily spinning its web.

'Eh?' The old man came to the floor level and adjusted his contact lenses. 'Aye, so it is! It's old Loony! 'E must have escaped from his quarters below.'

'So I gathered. Take him away, Joe, and don't ever let him come up here again. For that matter I think it would be a good idea if the Executive ordered his destruction. I can't understand what they were thinking of, allowing you to bring such an atrocious pet into your quarters.'

The janitor said nothing. He went to the corner, held out his hand, and immediately Loony deserted his web-weaving and ran up the old man's arm to his shoulder, there to poise content.

'Sorry if 'e caused trouble, doctor,' the janitor mumbled, heading back to the trapdoor. 'I promise it won't 'appen again if you'll not say anythin' to the Executive. Loony's the only companion I've got on this damned lonely job. 'Sides, there's a sort of sentimental value.'

'Because your son is an ace space pilot

8

and brought that disgusting insect back from Mars as a present for you?' Dr. Brunner laughed cynically. 'You are very easily pleased, Joe. As for the Executive, I shall ask them if that insect is really desirable in a place like this.'

'But doctor, I — '

'You can get below, Joe.'

Joe muttered something and then descended out of sight. Brunner considered the notes in his beefy hand.

'Dr. Brunner, do you think that was altogether fair?'

'Mmm? Fair?' Brunner looked up sharply, his dark eyes pinning the black-haired, straight-nosed Monica Adley. 'What precisely do you mean by that, Miss Adley?'

'I'm talking about Joe and his pet. He's right, you know. As a widower, his job is lonely — more lonely than for any of us. We're only here part of the time. He has six months non-stop as caretaker. That insect pet is little enough consolation.'

Brunner smiled wintrily. 'I am sure Joe would be glad to know he has a champion — especially one so charming. As far as

Loony goes, Miss Adley, I shall inform the Executive in the morning that I strongly recommend his destruction. That being settled, let us begin the evening's work. Mr. Calhoun — '

'Yes, doctor?' David Calhoun waited, a young and vigorous blond, far more like an athlete than an astronomer.

'You will assist me in the final computations on Neptune, checking our figures with the central computer. Kindly start up the reflector generator.'

Calhoun nodded and went across to the control panel that handled all the power for the observatory.

'You, Miss Adley, will continue your spectrographic analysis of the solar albedo reflecting from Neptune.'

Monica looked momentarily surprised. 'You will wish me to work here, then, beside you?'

'Since the spectrograph is in here that is a commendable deduction Miss Adley.' Brunner's heavy upper lip was somewhat sneering. 'I trust you will not find it irksome to work beside me? Or is it that you think I am deliberately preventing you from working in the room below where Mr. Calhoun will be busy with the computer?'

Monica flushed and Calhoun himself looked up sharply from the switch panel.

'That remark was entirely uncalled for, doctor!' Monica said curtly, flushing.

'Was it?' The cold smile was still there and Brunner's dark eyes shifted to Calhoun.

'You know damned well it was!' Calhoun himself snapped. 'In this confounded place everything is strictly business. That Miss Adley and I have happened to be alone in the room below on several occasions has merely been the outcome of duty.'

'Perhaps it would be as well, then, if you made your regard for each other a little less blatant, or at least reserved it for your off-duty moments. I have been aware for some time that your attachment for each other is far in excess of the needs of business. Henceforth, Miss Adley, you will work here beside me. Your duties, Mr. Calhoun, will either be confined to below, or else to such tasks that will enable me to keep an eye on you.'

'You — you *dare* to treat me like a schoolgirl!' Monica flamed. 'Tomorrow I'll ask the Executive to give me another position! You may be the head of the observatory, Dr. Brunner, but you can't direct people's lives for them!'

'Whilst you are under my authority you will do as I say, Miss Adley. It is as simple as that!'

'You're sure all this isn't occasioned by jealousy because you fancy Monica yourself?' David Calhoun demanded bluntly — and at that the big German turned and stared at him bleakly.

'A remark like that could bring about your dismissal, Mr. Calhoun!'

'All right — see if I care! If I go Monica will go too — that's how much we mean to each other!'

'Right!' Monica confirmed boldly.

Brunner looked from one to the other and then smiled sourly.

'Thank you for admitting your attachment, anyway. I will disregard your observation of a moment ago, Mr. Calhoun, and suggest you get down below immediately.'

Calhoun hesitated, his fists clenched — then with an angry look he swung away and descended the ladder into the computing and drawing room below. Here were housed all the machines for mathematical prediction and checking, photographic equipment, and drawing benches for the execution of space charts intended for interplanetary navigators.

In the observatory, Monica turned away slowly and went to the nearby spectrographic equipment. Brunner watched her go, then his eyes switched to Sasmo of Procyon. It would not do to say anything unpleasant to Sasmo; he was a being of poisonous politeness, which covered the tigerish cruelty inherited from his brilliant, soulless race.

'So far,' Brunner said patronizingly, 'I have been very satisfied with your drawings and calculations concerning the distribution of planets in the Procyon region, Sasmo — though how much can be attributed to your own astronomical genius and how much to the instruments you have been using, I don't know . . .'

'Do you mean, Dr. Brunner,' Sasmo asked, with his oddly deliberate tongue, 'that you secretly believe much of my work has been instinctively correct because of my ancestry?'

'Not exactly — but before your report goes to the Executive tomorrow I would be glad if you'd check your computations in the normal way. I do not doubt your observations because I know your brilliance, but the Executive may not be so easy to please. They must have proof from the readings of machines which they can understand.'

'I dislike my ability being questioned,' Sasmo said. 'And I dislike even more having to resort to inept machinery to prove me right!'

Brunner compressed his heavy lips and looked at the man from Procyon pensively. He was a small-built but extremely wide being, solid as cast iron, with an absolutely round and totally bald head. His eyes were large and green, his mouth little more than a scar. The general effect, combined with his ultra-thin nose, was decidedly startling.

'The machinery,' Brunner said, 'is not inept, and I must ask you to do as I order.'

'And if my calculations do not happen to agree with the machines?'

'But they *must* agree, Sasmo!'

'It does not always happen so. Scientists in the past have proven certain facts by their own figures, with which those calculating machines have been at variance. I do not trust machines: only myself.'

'Nevertheless, the order stands,' Brunner said.

The alien hesitated, then his scratch of a mouth parted in a thin smile.

'As you wish, doctor. I only hope that neither you nor anybody else will ever be foolish enough to infer that I am capable of making an astronomical mistake.'

With that Sasmo turned to the floor opening and descended below to join Calhoun at the computing machinery, though each was to work on a totally different astronomical problem. In the observatory above Brunner turned and watched the mighty reflector as it moved slowly under the influence of the electric motor driving it in synchronism with the Earth's revolution. Satisfied it was in order he looked towards Monica Adley.

'Are you ready for fitting the spectrograph connection, Miss Adley?'

'When you are, doctor.' Her voice was respectful, but icy.

Brunner went across to the switch panel and pulled a lever. Immediately there was a deep rumbling as the two hemispheres of roof parted and then began to slide down into their prearranged slots. In a moment or two the naked, starry sky was visible, high above the clouds that were gathered over the lower regions.

'We have a fine night for astronomy, Miss Adley,' Brunner commented. 'Let us hope it remains so for my study of Betelgeuse. Get the weather report, will you please?'

Monica crossed to the radio equipment and switched it on. Since weather reports were given continuously throughout the twenty-four hours on this particular waveband there was an immediate announcement.

'Weather forecast for April seventh, twenty-one ninety-one — time, nine hours fifteen. Depression centred over northern England will move southeastwards. Secondary will cross southern regions towards four a.m. bringing gales which may reach hurricane force. Until then weather in the southern and Metropolitan area will remain fair or fine with normal temperature. This is the Metropolitan Weather Bureau issuing — '

Monica switched off and Brunner gave a nod. 'Satisfactory enough. I'll have my Betelgeuse observations finished before four in the morning.'

Monica did not comment. She moved back silently towards the spectrographic equipment, until she suddenly found Brunner's powerful hand gripping her arm.

'What sort of a woman are you?' he asked bitterly. 'Is our work not exacting enough without you having to make it more difficult by showing no co-operation? Even my wife, who unhappily died on

Mars some years ago, helped me willingly no matter what my mood.'

'I am not your wife, Dr. Brunner. Kindly take your hand away from my arm!'

Brunner complied, grinning sardonically. 'I apologise. I merely ask, since we have to work together, that you adopt a more conciliatory attitude.'

'Why? It cannot influence our work.'

'I believe that it can, Miss Adley. Candidly, I find it very irksome having to address an assistant who never speaks unless compelled. You are not usually like this.'

'Until tonight you had never insulted me, Dr. Brunner.'

'Insulted you?' Brunner laughed heavily. 'Because of what I said about you and Calhoun? It's true, so why take offence?'

'When you are ready for the spectrographic analysis of Neptune, doctor, I am also.'

Brunner hesitated, searching Monica's coldly unresponsive good-looking face. He could read plain hatred of him in her eyes, yet in her tone there was nothing to which he could reasonably take exception.

'If you *were* my wife,' he said abruptly, 'I should make it my business to see you became more responsive when spoken to. My first wife knew better than to sulk.'

'I am *not* your wife, Dr. Brunner, and never shall be. As an astronomer I think you're at the top of your class; as a man I despise everything about you, and always have.'

Brunner grinned. 'That's more like it! And don't be too sure you won't be my second wife, either. I like them when they're hard to get!'

Monica looked after him fixedly as he returned to the reflector and settled in the chair that immediately overlooked the mercuroid mirror at the base of the telescope. It was as though she had suddenly realized something about Dr. Henry Brunner, and with the realization had come dread. Then his curt voice brought her back to reality.

'Spectrograph, Miss Adley! We are trained directly on Neptune.'

Immediately Monica closed the switch

that automatically transferred the light passing down the reflector through the prismatic channel input of the spectrograph. On the screen there came the spectrum of Neptune, and Monica studied it intently, making her notes meanwhile.

The fact that the light intake of the reflector was being deflected into the spectrographic equipment did not mean that there was no image of Neptune on the scanning mirror. There was, and quite a good one, too. The secret lay in the extraordinary light-gathering property of the mercuroid mirror, the latest conception of 2191 science.

In silence, his chair fixed to a long metal arm so that it jutted out over the mirror and enabled him to look down upon it, Brunner sat and studied the face of the penultimate world of the solar system. Every now and again he pressed the button on his chair arm and the long girder supporting him began to move — taking him to any part of the mirror which he desired. The snap of another switch opened a panel in the chair back and an elbow arm reached up and then lowered a microphone to within six inches of Brunner's mouth.

'You there, Calhoun?' he asked curtly, and from the room below, through a loudspeaker, Calhoun's voice came back.

'Waiting, Dr. Brunner.'

'Check back on the Incidental Segment. Studying it again I get a reading of four seven two, not four seven six. After that make sure that the lateral incidence balances.'

'Yes, doctor.'

So the evening's work began, and never for a moment did Dr. Brunner let up. He was a man of indefatigable energy and concentration once he started on his task and as long as he remained at his job he expected — perhaps rightly — everybody else to do likewise. Except Sasmo. He never felt he could order the man from Procyon to do the things he expected of his own race.

It was eleven-thirty when the session had finished. Monica's spectrographic work was complete. Down below in the computing department Calhoun was busy checking the figures and angles that had been barked at him through three long hours whilst the mighty telescope had followed Neptune in his slow perambulation across the still cloudless sky . . . Now was the moment for relaxation.

'I think,' Dr. Brunner said, easing himself from the telescopic chair and flexing cramped limbs, 'that it is time we had some coffee. Where's that fool Joe?'

He strode across to the bell-push, pausing as Monica said:

'Not for me, doctor, thank you.'

Brunner looked at her with his sharp, dark eyes. 'What do you mean — not for you?'

'I was referring to the coffee. Now the session is over I would prefer not to delay any further. Besides, I have some important work to finish at home before I retire.'

Brunner pressed the bell-push and grinned cynically. 'Very odd how this important work has suddenly manifested itself. As a rule you are only too willing to join in our final coffee group before leaving.'

'Matters,' Monica said, putting aside her spectrographic notes into the folder, 'are not exactly as they were, doctor.'

He lounged across to her, hands in trouser pockets, a quizzical look on his sensual face.

'So you still think it necessary to exhibit this ridiculous hostility towards me?'

'It's not hostility, doctor. I simply prefer to confine myself to my work and then leave . . . ' Monica handed over the spectrograph folder and then turned away to where her coat and hat were hanging. Brunner watched her in silence, reflecting that the biscuit colour of her coat set off her dark hair and pink-and-white skin to perfection.

'Did you ring, doctor?' The head and shoulders of Joe appeared from the floor well. Brunner turned and looked at him.

'Of course I did, you old fool. You don't suppose the bell rang by itself, do you? Fetch coffee and sandwiches for three and be quick about it.'

'Three, doctor? Four usually, isn't it, seeing that Mr. Sasmo doesn't drink coffee?'

'None for me, thanks,' came Calhoun's voice from below. 'I'm getting off home.'

'How very natural,' Brunner sneered, glaring at Monica as she set her hat in position. 'You and Calhoun depart together and show your childish sulkiness by refusing to drink the final coffee with me.'

Monica turned to the floor well as the bewildered janitor's head and shoulders disappeared.

'Good night, Dr. Brunner,' she said briefly, and began the descent which took her out of sight.

Brunner muttered something and went across to the desk to check the records Monica had made. It annoyed him considerably to discover at first glance that her work had been flawlessly done. Nothing would have suited him better at the moment than to have reason to find fault.

'The calculations you asked for, doctor.'

Brunner gave the slightest of starts and took the folder handed to him. Then his gaze travelled up to Calhoun's young, good-looking face.

'It is to be hoped that these are correct, Mr. Calhoun.'

'They are. If not, the Executive know where to contact me. In the morning I shall ask for a transfer as I find the conditions here no longer amicable. Good night, Dr. Brunner — '

'A moment, Calhoun!'

Calhoun hesitated in his forward stride and then returned to the chief's desk. Without looking up, Brunner said:

'Since you have so suddenly decided to ask for a transfer, Mr. Calhoun, I must ask that you leave your work here in order first. You have forty-eight hours in which to check over the mathematical readings on Uranus and Saturn made in the last two months.'

Calhoun started. 'But that's impossible, doctor! Those figures need checking to the last detail. Space travellers' lives depend on their accuracy. To check everything in forty-eight hours is impossible.'

'I do not think it is, Mr. Calhoun, and I expect it to be done.' Brunner glanced up briefly. 'Possibly, had you spent more time with the computers and less with Miss Adley you might not have so much work to catch up.'

Calhoun flushed and he tightened his big fists, but he had the good sense not to hit his chief in the jaw, as he felt very much inclined to do. Such an action as that could have landed him in jail for a couple of years and lost him his entire career.

'I'll see everything is finished to time,' he said stiffly, and without another word he took his departure. Brunner watched him go and then shrugged to himself.

'Maybe it is time we had a change of staff, anyway,' he muttered, 'particularly in regard to a woman assistant. Monica Adley is evidently too difficult to handle. Maybe one with less efficiency and more co-operation is what is needed.' He grinned a little to himself, then it faded again as old Joe came into view with one cup of coffee. He put it down on the desk.

'Only you for it tonight, doctor,' he commented. 'First time that's happened, isn't it?'

'Has to be a first time for everything, Joe . . . and a last.'

Joe scratched the back of his head dubiously, quite unable to make anything of the remark.

'Mr. Sasmo down below?' Brunner asked, stirring the coffee.

'Yes, doctor. He was just — Oh, here 'e is now.'

'All right — get back below. And say goodbye to that damned gossamer spider of yours. It'll be dead by this time tomorrow!'

Joe did not say anything. He shambled across the observatory, passing Sasmo on the way. The alien did not even glance at him. As usual he was concentrated solely upon himself and his own accomplishments.

'The figures you asked me to check concerning the Procyon System are now complete, Dr. Brunner,' he announced. 'I am sure the Executive will have no fault to find with them.'

Brunner took the file handed to him and put it on the desk.

'All right, Sasmo, I'll take your word for it.'

'If there *is* an error,' Sasmo added, 'it can only be attributed to the machines, not to me. I am never wrong — at least, not as regards Procyon.'

'Nothing like being modest, is there?' Brunner gave his hard grin.

'I do not know what you mean by that, doctor. I have none of the emotions common to Earth people. I am simply an infallible mental machine as far as astronomy is concerned. However, I appreciate that, if an error appears it will be *I* who will get the blame and not the machines. What do you suppose my punishment would be?'

'Removal from the Astronomical Service, my friend — and in a case like yours that would be fatal. It's the only thing for which you are ideally suited.'

The man of Procyon reflected, his square face giving no hint of his thoughts. Then finally he inclined his bullet head in a slight bow.

'That is all you require for tonight, doctor?'

'That is all, yes. You can go . . . Might I enquire the reason for your almost indecent haste? Usually you stay behind to check your own special astronomical notes.'

'Tonight there is a heavy storm approaching doctor. I can sense it. I would prefer to be at ground level when it breaks.'

'Yes,' Brunner growled. 'A gale warning was given not so long ago.'

'As usual,' Sasmo said, 'I do not require scientific instruments in order to be informed of elemental changes. My nervous system is such that I can apprehend them in advance.'

That this was true Brunner had good reason to know so he did not comment. He merely nodded briefly as with his stiff, formal little bow the man of Procyon went on his way and disappeared through the floor trap.

Pondering to himself Brunner drank his coffee slowly and then lighted his pipe. Getting to his feet he strolled across to the roof ladder. In a few minutes he had descended it and then stood on the narrow railed parapet, which marked the uttermost limit of the wide channels into which the hemispheres of roof had dropped.

At the moment the April night was deadly calm: there was not even a breeze. But over to the north the clear dome of heaven was masked by a deeper darkness than the night, probably the secondary impression moving southeastwards as predicted by the weather bureau. It would be some time before the sky was completely clouded over, time in which Brunner could make his required study of the giant Betelgeuse.

Down below in the observatory old Joe perked his head above the floor trap and looked around him. When at last he caught a glimpse of Dr. Brunner's legs high up on the parapet of the roof, Joe finished his ascent of the ladder and crossed to the abandoned coffee cup. Since it was empty it was logical to clear it away.

With it in his hand he walked back to the floor trap and his shortsighted gaze failed to observe that once again his gossamer-spider pet had escaped from below and was already weaving weird and delightful patterns in a far corner of the observatory.

Brunner remained for quite ten minutes on the parapet, glad of the fresh air after the clammy, artificial heat below. At length he turned his gaze from surveying the glitter of the stars and considered instead the view two miles below. It was absolutely clear tonight — a patchwork of grey and bright spots of light stretching out as far as the horizon. Even the English Channel was visible as a brighter greyness in the gloom.

Then Brunner's attention was attracted by something else — two fireflies of light moving through the night and finally stopping at the base of the mighty observatory column thrusting up out of the void. Evidently somebody's car had arrived. Brunner frowned as he wondered whom it might be and then he began to descend again into the observatory.

At this same moment David Calhoun stepped from the shaft elevator and went quickly through Joe's quarters towards the computing room.

'Back again so soon, Mr. Calhoun?' Joe

asked, in surprise. 'Thought you'd finished for tonight.'

'So did I, Joe, but I forgot some special
papers that need checking . . . '

Joe nodded and returned to the study
of his newspaper. The door closed behind
Calhoun as he went into the next
department. Outside, the silence of the
night was disturbed by the first puffs of
breeze in advance of the secondary
depression . . .

2

Death at the Observatory

The phone in Monica Adley's apartment was ringing stridently. At first, as she lay asleep, Monica imagined that she was dreaming, then as it dawned upon her that this was the genuine article, she aroused herself quickly, threw on her robe, and raced into the lounge. Even as she glanced sleepily at the clock — which showed 3.30 — she found herself wondering vaguely who could want her at this hour. Probably a wrong number —

'Yes? Monica Adley speaking.'

'This is Joe, Miss Adley. Can you come right away to the observatory? I've already phoned for Mr. Calhoun and Mr. Sasmo and they'll be 'ere immediately.'

'But — but what for? What's wrong, Joe?' The last trace of sleep vanished from Monica's brain. 'Something happened?'

'Yes, miss, an' I don't know what to do about it. I don't want to ring the Executive chief till I hear what you others have to say. It's Dr. Brunner — 'e's been murdered.'

Monica started. '*Murdered*, did you say?'

'That's what it looks like to me — '

'I'll come right away, Joe — just as fast as I can get dressed.'

Which took Monica exactly ten minutes; then jamming on her hat and whirling her light-coloured dust coat about her she hurried from her apartment and out to the yard where stood the garages. In another five minutes her car was speeding down the brightly lighted but mainly deserted city streets until at last she reached the area of Observatory Park. Here, as she alighted from her car at the base of the stupendous observatory column, she noticed for the first time that the wind was blowing at gale force and spots of rain were falling. In the enclosed region where her apartment building stood she had not noticed it particularly.

Bowing her head to the gale and holding on to her hat she struggled across the area to the column entrance doors. As she went she noticed nearby the cars of Sasmo and Calhoun, so evidently they had got here before her. Then she was inside. the column's main hall and stepped into the automatic elevator. Pressing the button she sent herself whirling to the top of the stupendous length and then stepped out into the softly lighted main corridor of the summit. Here there was a deep, over-powering roaring sound — the onslaught of a hurricane wind vastly increased in power at this great height.

Joe was not in his usual department so Monica quickly ascended the ladder into the observatory. Here the lights were blazing and the roof had been closed. Joe Calhoun, and Sasmo were standing close together, looking down on the sprawled body of Dr. Brunner beside the huge reflector.

'What's happened?' Monica demanded, hurrying forward, and at the sound of her voice the three turned.

'Obvious, isn't it?' Calhoun asked quietly.

Monica moved to his side, then changed her position so as to get a clearer view of the body on the floor. Resting against the massive bulk of the reflector's main eyepiece Monica studied the fallen Brunner intently.

He lay face upwards, a savage, discoloured gash across the right side of his forehead. His collar had been wrenched open, leaving his tie streaming, and upon the thick flesh of his throat were distinct marks as though from manual strangulation. The worst feature were his eyes — staring upwards in a glaze of fear as though in his last moment he had seen something horribly not of this world.

'It's — ghastly,' Monica muttered, turning away.

It was Calhoun who spoke after a long pause.

'Fact remains, Monica, that he's dead — and from the look of things death was either caused by that smack on the head or from being choked. Joe, you'd better tell Miss Adley what you told me.'

Joe looked uncomfortable. He was in

pyjamas and a somewhat faded dressing gown.

'Must have been around three o'clock when I 'eard the most frightful cry! Just like an animal that's been wounded, it was. Then I 'eard a lot of bumpin' and bangin', only with the wind blowin' so 'ard I couldn't make out whether the noise was comin' from in 'ere or whether it was the gale outside. Anyway, I got up fast as I could an' found Dr. Brunner lyin' 'ere. Didn't take me above a few seconds to find 'e was dead. So I did the only thing possible — rang you all up. I'm not takin' all this responsibility by meself.'

'Who closed the roof?' Monica looked up at it.

'I did,' Calhoun told her. 'Rain was coming in and the gale was making the devil of a racket.'

Silence again, save for a curious far-distant twanging note caused by the contraction and expansion of the column as it adapted itself to the hurricane. But here in the observatory everything was steady — rock steady.

'There is nothing we can do about this,' Sasmo said at length. 'The fact that Dr. Brunner is dead — which I for my part find decidedly welcome — means that, by your law each one of us comes under suspicion. Therefore let us have the law here and start the process of elimination.'

Calhoun nodded slowly and then turned to the telephone. Raising it he said curtly, 'Get me the police . . . '

Which was enough to cause the four to stay in the observatory until daybreak. Once the police arrived, their questioning was ceaseless and ruthless, as was the medical analysis made by the police surgeon. Grey daylight was coming over the wet windy landscape when at length Calhoun and Monica emerged from the column's entrance hall.

'Nasty business,' Calhoun said grimly, and Monica gave a troubled nod.

'Have to see how it works out, that's all. What did you gather from the police proceedings?'

'I gathered that they haven't the vaguest idea who did it — as yet. My only hope is that they don't pick on the wrong person in order to have a culprit and so save their faces.'

Monica sighed. 'Though I shouldn't say it, of course, I must admit I'm not sorry that Dr. Brunner has been — er — is no longer in charge. The position ought to fall to you as next in line.'

'Granting I don't get pushed in jail, yes.'

Monica looked surprised. 'Why on earth should you be suspected more than the rest of us?'

'There's a reason, Monica, and one it won't be easy to get out of, either . . . ' Calhoun hesitated momentarily, then, 'I came back to the observatory after leaving last night.'

'You came *back*? But what for?'

'Some papers. That's perfectly genuine, but what has me bothered is how to prove it was genuine.' They began walking to their respective cars and it was Monica who spoke next.

'Dave, I've been thinking — I don't like you taking risks with your liberty when there's such circumstantial evidence against you. Once the police know you came back here they'll nail you'

'I know.' Calhoun shrugged. 'What am I supposed to do about it?'

'Of yourself, nothing — unless it's under instructions. What about calling on Adam Quirke?'

Calhoun was silent, running his fingers pensively along the wet frame of the car's wing.

'No guarantee he'd bother with a thing like this,' he said at length. 'Quirke is a specialist in scientific crime — not plain murder by a bash on the head like this is.'

'Quirke,' Monica said deliberately, 'is interested in anything provided it exercises his talents. And whether he is or not I am going to see him rather than have you gamble with the police — ' Monica stopped suddenly, sheer horror crossing her face. 'Dave, you didn't do it, did you?'

He looked at her sourly. 'What kind of a chump do you think I am? Of course I didn't! I don't say I wouldn't have liked to, but I'm entirely innocent.'

'That's good enough for me. Will you

see Mr. Quirke, or shall I? For that matter we could go together.'

Calhoun thought for a moment, then decided. 'I'd sooner you saw him yourself: you'll be able to spin a better tale about me when I'm not there. Let me know how you get on . . . How's that?'

'I'll go on my way home,' Monica promised — which was exactly what she did. Quirke, however, was not available at so early an hour, so all Monica could do was make an appointment through the electric tape-recording gadget on the door, and then continue on her way to her apartment.

When at length she started out again, still feeling somewhat muzzy through lack of sleep and merciless questioning, it was ten o'clock. The morning papers and early tv and radio bulletins were already blasting forth the news of Brunner's murder, chiefly because anything which happened in or around the lofty observatory was always a safe bet for a news item . . .

Adam Quirke's residence was a detached house in the city centre, encircled with scientific gadgets, by which the somewhat eccentric scientific detective was able to watch, listen to, and generally analyse all those who called upon him long before they came into his actual presence. And this morning was no exception. The moment Monica began to advance up the drive of the house the photo-electric beams which her body impeded started up the 'gadget department' and the analysing equipment went into action.

Quirke himself surveyed the pin-sharp close-up of Monica as she rang the front door bell, then he looked over the instruments.

'Mm, fair enough,' he commented after a moment. 'Dark haired, apparently quickwitted, her pulses racing more than usual. Look at that heartbeat register, Molly! The girl's excited or else nervous. Five feet five, trimly dressed — Right!' He moved the lever at his side and automatically the front door opened.

Monica stood looking into the hall and, even as the laboratory indicators had shown, her pulses were racing. There was something quite scarifying about Quirke's abode.

'Do come in, madam,' boomed a hidden loudspeaker. 'Straight down the hall to the door marked 'Private'.'

Monica obeyed, but she jumped a little when another p.e.c. beam caused the door to shut adamantly behind her . . . Then she went on, tapped on the door marked 'Private', and entered. She had rather expected an office with all the appurtenances thereto; instead she beheld a fully equipped laboratory and quite the biggest man she had ever seen advancing towards her in welcome.

'Good morning, Miss Adley — It *is* Miss Adley?'

'Yes, yes, I'm Miss Adley.'

'Splendid! I received your appointment satisfactorily. Make yourself comfortable . . . '

Rather uneasily Monica settled in the hide armchair, which appeared distinctly incongruous amidst the scientific equipment.

'My secretary,' Quirke explained, nodding towards the fair-haired, grey-eyed, still twentyish girl who had just come into view with her notebook in hand. 'Miss Brayson — otherwise the light of my life.'

Monica nodded a quick acknowledgment and then fumbled needlessly with her handbag. She did not know why she felt nervous, unless it was that Adam Quirke's huge dimensions overawed her. Certainly it was massive — six feet nine in height and well up to twenty-two stone in weight. His face was too large and round, capped with an untidy mane of white hair: His age was a doubtful quantity but from his milk-and-roses complexion he could have been anything between thirty-five and fifty-five. Then the eyes — shrewd, merry, intense china-blue. Monica realised they were watching her appraisingly.

'Shall we get to business?' Quirke suggested, and eased his colossal nether end on to the nearby bench so that he sat with legs dangling like an over-fat schoolboy.

'I'm sorry,' Monica apologised. 'I feel sort of muddled up inside . . . It's about the observatory murder Mr. Quirke. It probably doesn't come within your province but I wondered if you would interest yourself in it.'

'Any particular reason why I should?'

'Well, yes — the fact that the police may probably nail the young man to whom I — er — Well, not yet, but it will come.'

'So will Christmas,' Quirke said solemnly, and then he exploded into a hurricane of laughter. It had such violence and was so prolonged that Monica began to expect hysteria. Not so Molly Brayson, the secretary. She waited calmly, an eyebrow lifted, until the storm should pass. When it did it was abrupt, and Quirke was himself again except for the tears dancing in his bright eyes.

'Upon my soul, Molly,' he panted, 'I get wittier every day!'

'Yes, A.Q.,' Molly agreed, in a dead, mechanical voice.

'You mean,' Quirke said, looking at Monica, 'that you are hoping to become engaged to the young man whom you are afraid the police will arrest.'

'Yes!' Monica looked relieved. 'That's it.'

'Meaning Mr. Calhoun, I take it? I am sure the estimable Sasmo of Procyon cannot be your — er — intended.'

Monica looked surprised for a moment. 'Oh, of course you have the names from the television, or newspapers! I'd forgotten.'

'The names from the papers and the facts from the Commissioner of the Interplanetary and Metropolitan Police. He is a very old friend of mine.'

'I see. Then I hardly need to give you any details . . . '

Quirke grinned widely. 'My dear Miss Adley, I am not a thought reader, whatever other qualifications I may be presumed to possess. Tell me everything in your own way and rest assured I am entirely sympathetic. Ready, Molly?'

'Ready, A.Q.,' and Molly Brayson sat at a nearby table and tossed her notebook upon it.

'I don't really know a great deal, Mr. Quirke. I was awakened around half past three this morning by a phone call from

Joe, the observatory caretaker-janitor. He said Dr. Brunner had been murdered and would I go right away. I did. Mr. Calhoun and Mr. Sasmo were there before me. We sent for the police and they questioned us with ruthless efficiency. Then Dave — that's Mr. Calhoun — told me he went back last night to the observatory for some papers and that the police might construe that into some kind of excuse for him having murdered Brunner ... I decided, with Dave's assent, to come and see you.'

'Thank you for the compliment, Miss Adley. With my dimensions I'm sure you will have no difficulty in seeing me! Eh, Molly?'

The laboratory quivered; Quirke rocked back and forth dangerously on the bench edge — then again the calm. Molly Brayson waited, her grey eyes coldly indifferent.

'Why be convinced the police will only pick on Calhoun?' Quirke asked abruptly.

'I've just given you the reasons, Mr. Quirke. Because of the papers for which he returned — '

'To be sure, but I am certain the police will also have noted the not inconsiderable bloodstain on your coat sleeve there, granting it is the same coat you wore last night.'

'Blood — ?' Monica looked horrified, then brought round her arm to investigate.

'The other one,' Quirke told her, and after some manoeuvre she managed to discover a fair-sized brownish stain clearly visible on the light, biscuit colour of her coat, and examined the defilement more closely.

'*Can't* be blood,' she insisted, looking up. 'I haven't cut myself, or anything. Paint, probably.'

Quirke slid from the bench and held out a fat hand. 'With your permission, Miss Adley?'

With a troubled frown Monica handed over the coat and Quirke gave it to the waiting Molly. With an air of complete efficiency Molly went to work with the Benzedrine test and then returned.

'Blood,' she said phlegmatically. 'And human blood at that.'

'Group?' A.Q. asked, and received an injured glance.

'After all, A.Q., I didn't have time to make the agglutin test.'

'My apologies.' Suddenly Quirke's china-blue eyes were hard as he handed the coat back to Monica. 'Blood it is, Miss Adley. Any suggestions?'

Monica was looking bewildered. 'None! I just don't understand it — I don't even know if it was on the sleeve when the police questioned us tonight. I've been in such a whirl I haven't paid any particular attention to my clothes.'

Silence. Monica slowly got into her coat again, though her expression was such that something unclean was enveloping her.

'Tell me,' Quirke mused, 'did you touch the body of Dr. Brunner at all?'

'Great heavens, no! I just looked at him — nothing more.'

'Interesting,' Quirke commented, fondling his florid bow-tie. 'You can take it for granted, Miss Adley, that that bloodstain will have been observed by the police, and they are expert enough to know the difference between blood and paint — so there would be little use in your not wearing that coat from here on.'

'Maybe not, but I can't bear to have it near me until it has been cleaned. I feel nauseated as it is having to wear it.'

'Then don't,' Quirke said cheerfully. 'Leave your coat here and I will do two things — completely analyse the stain and fix the blood group to which it belongs. I will also let you have the coat back spotlessly clean. You, Molly, will now put a sign on the front door — 'Adam Quirke, Dyer and Cleaner'.'

The small instruments of the laboratory vibrated with the bronchial explosions of Quirke's laughter; then at last he dabbed his eyes with a baby sheet and said briefly, 'Coffee, Molly. We need a break . . . '

'Yes, A.Q.' Molly disappeared into another region of the laboratory, taking Monica's coat with her. Quirke surveyed Monica's neat blouse and business-like skirt and then said: 'Molly will lend you a coat in which to get home. Your dimensions are pretty similar. One of mine certainly wouldn't do.'

Monica smiled and then had to laugh with Quirke as he quaked like a monstrous Falstaff over his obscure joke. Like many a person before her, Monica found it hard to credit that such a mountainous buffoon as this could possibly possess one of the keenest scientific minds in the world. So far Monica had not guessed the simple truth — that Quirke disarmed everybody with his elephantine humour whilst he gave himself time to think.

'Had you a liking for Dr. Brunner?' he asked presently.

'None.' Monica's mouth set harshly. 'I admired his ability as an astronomer and mathematician — but as a man he was loathsome. Or at least he seemed so to me, as a woman. I can't say whether men felt the same about him, but I *do* know he was not liked.'

'Had you some special reason for disliking him more than anybody else?'

'He . . . He was the voluptuous type. I'll let it go at that.'

'You would, in fact, consider the world

a sweeter place for his absence?'

'Definitely!'

'And did others know of your dislike of him?'

'All of them, yes. Things got so bad last night I was intending this morning to ask the Executive to transfer me. I could not have tolerated another session with Dr. Brunner at any price. You can't imagine how I felt when alone with him in the main observatory. Not so much what he said but the way he looked at me — Possessive, cynical,' Monica averted her face and Quirke sat on the nearby hardwood chair and puffed gently. Then Molly returned with three coffees and handed two of them over.

'So things reached a crisis last night, did they?' Quirke stirred his coffee daintily. 'The police will have made a note of *that* too, I'm afraid.'

'I suppose so,' Monica admitted, sighing. 'Brunner seemed to get on all our nerves last night. Dave had a brush with him. Then there was almost a row with Sasmo — and even the poor old janitor got it in the neck because of Loony.'

Quirke stopped stirring his coffee. 'Loony? I have not had any reference to that.'

'No, you won't have had. It's really quite trivial. Loony is a gossamer-spider, and Joe's special pet.'

'Ah, yes! Charming insects imported from Mars.'

Monica nodded. 'Joe let his stray into the observatory and Brunner raised the devil with him. Said the observatory was no place for the spider and he'd have the Executive order its destruction. That would have been today, had Brunner lived.'

'From which,' Quirke commented, 'we may infer that Dr. Brunner was not exactly the right type to be the leader of a Sunday school movement. It would also appear, unless Sasmo and the janitor have something incriminating about them — such as a bloodstain or a return for papers — that you and Mr. Calhoun are the two on whom the police will concentrate their attention. I think your coming to me was very wise, Miss Adley.'

Monica flushed a little. 'I'm glad you

say that, Mr. Quirke. Dave wasn't at all sure that I should do it. Right now I think you should know that *I* did not murder Dr. Brunner. I left him drinking coffee in the observatory — or at least about to — and then I went straight home, finished off a few notes, and so to bed. Next thing I knew the telephone was ringing.'

'And are you in a position to prove all this, young lady?'

'Well — er — I don't think I am. You know how it is when you go home late every night, when it's part of your job. Nobody to see you come and go — No I'm afraid I can't prove it.'

'Pity,' Quirke said. "specially considering the bloodstain on your sleeve. However, don't let things get you down. I'll start the ball rolling immediately.'

Monica was not quite sure whether this was a dismissal or not, but since her coffee was finished she got to her feet and then looked about her.

'You did mention something about a coat — ?'

'Ah, yes!' Quirke had surged from his

chair and gave a glance towards Molly. 'Light of my life, you have two coats here, have you not, in case of rain? That being so, will you kindly lend one to Miss Adley — Case of rain!' Quirke broke off, bellowing and spluttering until it seemed he must collapse from apoplexy. 'In *this* country!'

The laboratory trembled to his hurricane laughter as Molly fetched one of her overcoats from the nearby hook. By the time Monica had slipped the garment on, Quirke was just about recovering.

'Leave everything to me, Miss Adley.' He was still choking and gasping with inner merriment. 'The moment I've anything worthwhile to report I'll contact you — You're on the phone, of course. The number?'

'Central seven eight two.'

Molly made a note of it and Quirke held out his hand. 'Till next time then, Miss Adley.'

Nobody saw Monica to the door. It opened for her, as did the front door when she went down the hall. Quirke stood looking at her reflection in the television mirror until she was out of sight down the drive, then he turned to Molly.

'Any ideas, light of my life?'

'At this stage, A.Q., none at all. She seems a decent enough girl, and pretty capable, I should think.'

'Just as long as she isn't capable of *anything*,' Quirke mused.

'About this coat — ' Molly picked it up. 'Want me to give it a thorough analysis? The bloodstain, I mean?'

'Yes, you'd better do that. In the meantime I think I should have a word with the Commissioner and see how the land lies.'

'You won't need me for that, then?'

'I always need you, light of my life — but don't let my wife know.'

Grinning and gulping Quirke pulled off his laboratory smock and then struggled into a huge grey overcoat. A hat he never wore: his bush of white hair was an identification mark in itself — and as usual it secured him a prompt audience with the Commissioner of the Interplanetary and Metropolitan Police.

'Sit down and make yourself at home,

Quirke.' The Commissioner shook hands and then motioned to a chair. 'What can I do for you?'

'What you could do for me, Commissioner, wouldn't cover a postage stamp. It's the other way round . . . I'm working on the Dr. Brunner murder.'

'Oh — I see. Just like that, eh?'

'I'm a free agent, Commissioner, to work where and when I choose. You ought to be glad: you shout quick enough when you get out of your depth — you and those so-called backroom boys who think they know all the answers.'

'Ninety percent of 'em, anyway,' the Commissioner retorted. 'Trouble is, Mr. Quirke, you steal our thunder once you start. And anyway, this isn't a puzzling case — quite straightforward, murder from a blow on the head. Nothing in it.'

'The head, or the case?' Quirke rumbled and shook with inner merriment and the Commissioner waited in cold impatience for the attack to subside.

'Nothing scientific, anyhow,' the Commissioner said at last, raking through the pile of papers on the desk. 'I don't see why I should gratify you with our confidential reports, but I suppose I shall have to.'

'No doubt of it. If you don't want my aid now you probably will before you're finished. I don't incline to the theory that this is an ordinary blow-on-the-nut murder, my friend.'

'But it is. The surgeon himself says so. Death caused by a blow from a blunt instrument.'

Quirke groaned. '*That* again! When will the police drop that 'oodunit term and talk like adult men? Blunt instrument indeed!'

'And,' the Commissioner added, with a gleam in his eye, 'we are about to arrest the murderer.'

'About to? Why the procrastination?'

'Not much procrastination when the murder was only committed last night. We've had to check up on the details concerning David Calhoun. He's our man.'

'Because he returned to the observatory for papers?'

'Oh, you know then?'

'Certainly. Miss Adley, also of the observatory, started me off on investigating this business. And when you've finished scratching over those papers like an agitated fowl maybe we can get to business.'

With a suppressed calm the Commissioner yanked a sheet of parchment from the lake around him and handed it over. Quirke took it and read:

April 8, 2191.
Post Mortem Report on
Henry Brunner Deceased

In my considered opinion one of two causes brought about the death of Henry Brunner. It could either have been the severe blow on the forehead which fractured the frontal bone of the skull and also caused sever laceration above the right eyebrow — a blow inflicted by a blunt instrument and in itself enough to cause death; or it could have resulted from manual strangulation, there being obvious thumb and finger marks on the flesh of the throat. Even both causes could have been contributory to death. The body had been dead for about two hours when I was called in to make an examination.

Arnold Carter,
Surgeon to I. and M.
Police Dept.

'Mm,' Quirke said, handing back the report and then sitting in moody silence.

'No getting past that!' The Commissioner slapped his hand down on the report. 'Carter never makes a mistake.'

'That, Commissioner, is a dam'fool remark, if I may say so. *Everybody* makes mistakes sometimes — including myself. Thumb and fingermarks on Brunner's neck, eh? What's your theory about it?'

'That the murderer — Calhoun, we think — attacked Brunner by a stranglehold to begin with, failed in his objective, and finally had to use other means. So he battered Brunner with some blunt instrument, which he took away with him.'

'Motive?'

'Just plain, unvarnished hatred of the man. Far as I could make out from questioning Sasmo of Procyon and

Calhoun himself there was something bordering on a row last night at the observatory. Brunner made himself too pleasant to Miss Adley and Calhoun didn't like it. Evidently he came back later and squared things up. I haven't questioned Miss Adley yet apart from the others. I'm giving you the information our men dug out of the four last night in the observatory before they were allowed to go home.'

'And what about Sasmo and the janitor?'

'The janitor is a doubtful quantity, since he is always on the premises and had the time and opportunity — but against that we have to remember that he's getting an old man, and that he could have so thoroughly dealt with a powerfully built man in the prime of life, like Brunner, is most unlikely.'

'Unlikely or otherwise he had motive — and a strong one.'

'I suppose you're referring to that insect pet which Brunner said he'd have destroyed? Hardly enough to warrant murder, A.Q., and you know it.'

'And what about Sasmo?'

'Airtight alibi. When he left the observatory he went to the Interplanetary Club on Hundredth Street and stayed there until nearly half past three. Spent the time in the club library making notes from several of the books. I've checked up on that and there seems to be no doubt of it. Certainly Sasmo is one person who could not employ a double. There's nobody on Earth who looks exactly as he looks. He's a queer bird all the same,' the Commissioner went on, thinking. 'I'd just been looking at the sound-film record of the interrogation before you arrived — and if there's one person I can't weigh up it's Sasmo. Maybe just because he's an alien.'

'Any objection to my seeing that interrogation film?'

'Not in the least. Come into the projection room . . . '

Quirke struggled to his feet and breathing like a grampus he lumbered after the Commissioner — out of the office, down the corridor, and into the projection theatre. Afterwards, for the next hour, he was a silent witness of the sound-film made of the questioning of the suspects. By this means the modern Interplanetary and Metropolitan could often throw new light on a problematical situation by seeing the set-up over and over again and hearing the words spoken endlessly.

Not that Quirke took much interest in the questions and answers. Most of his attention was concentrated on the observatory itself, every detail as brilliant as crystal as the ever-watchful lens moved from place to place and up and down, zooming occasionally to some far corner and then retreating again.

There was Brunner still lying on the floor beside the reflector. There was Monica Adley answering questions and unconsciously revealing that bloodstain on her sleeve as she moved about. There was the voluble David Calhoun protesting his innocence, and the inscrutable, block-like Sasmo of Procyon looking on and betraying absolutely nothing from his expression.

'As I understand it,' Quirke said

presently, 'young Calhoun did not admit that he returned to the observatory last night for certain papers. It isn't in this interrogation film, anyhow. Yet you seemed to know all about it when I referred to it.'

'The janitor told us,' the Commissioner responded. 'And the fact that Calhoun suppressed it shows he'd something to hide. In another hour or less, he'll be under arrest . . . '

Silence, and gradually the film came to its close. The lights came up and the two men sat thinking and smoking.

'Satisfied?' the Commissioner asked.

'Not by any means, but thanks for the movie show. If you take my advice, Commissioner — as you've often done in the past — you will hold your hand before clapping a murder charge on Calhoun. There's a great deal more in this than meets the eye. For instance, where's the weapon with which Calhoun was supposed to have battered Brunner?'

'We haven't found it yet, but we shall.'

'You'd better. You can't accuse a man of using a blunt instrument and then not produce the instrument. Secondly, why lay it on so thick for poor Calhoun when Monica Adley is quite as much a suspect as he is?'

'Why should she be? She didn't return to the observatory once she'd left it for the night. We have the janitor's word for that.'

'Why take the janitor's word for everything when he too is suspect? Motive, remember! Oh I know all that business about him being an old man but he might have found a way had he wanted. You're being too heavy-handed, Commissioner. Go through each suspect with a toothcomb before making an arrest: that's my advice.'

The Commissioner's big jaw set stubbornly. 'We're satisfied with the evidence we have, A.Q. As for Monica Adley, she's about the least suspicious person in the group.'

'You surprise me! Even with that bloodstain on her sleeve?'

'I wondered if you knew about that,' the Commissioner remarked dryly.

'More than that, man, I'm having the

bloodstain analysed. I thought you'd do the same.'

'We don't consider it relevant insofar that there is no proof that Miss Adley returned to the observatory. That is the vital point. Since she did not return to the observatory the bloodstain probably has some other explanation. Besides, Miss Adley would never have been able to overpower Brunner and batter him like that. No, she's right out of it.'

Quirke sighed. 'Have it as you will, Commissioner.'

'I intend to. I can't play around with fanciful theories, A.Q., and take all the time I like examining every little detail under the microscope. The I and M Executives demand quick action. The inquest has already been adjourned pending further inquiry and we can't hold things up indefinitely.'

'Suppose,' Quirke said, 'it was somebody right outside the four connected with the observatory who finished off Brunner? Have you examined his personal life at all?'

'To the last detail. His private life was

not a pleasant one in that it revealed him to be a pretty brutal and licentious sort of man. Women of all ages abounded in his non-professional life but apparently no men. None of those women could have done the job. It was a man of considerable strength. Also, remember that nobody could get at him except by the column elevator, and whoever stepped off that elevator would be seen by the janitor. That is where the business is unique. The observatory being two miles in the air nobody could climb up the outside of the column either — and certainly not a woman.'

'Ever heard of a helicopter?' Quirke grinned.

'I thought of that and a descent through the open observatory roof — but last night about the time of Brunner's death there was a violent gale raging. No helicopter in the world could have made a successful approach to the column summit.'

Quirke stubbed out his cigarette, then: 'The thumb and finger marks on Brunner's neck. Weren't they clear enough for prints to be taken?'

'Unfortunately, no. Probably glove prints, anyway.'

'Having got precisely nowhere so far,' Quirke said, fighting his way to his feet and breathing hard, 'I may as well transfer my affections to what the crime novelists call 'the scene of the crime. Any objection?'

'Be all the same if I had,' the Commissioner growled. 'But understand this, Quirke, I'm resolved on one thing: David Calhoun is going to be arrested and I'm more than sure that in the end we'll dig up enough evidence to convict him.'

'And if you don't?'

'We shall!'

'If you don't,' Quirke said deliberately, 'you will be the laughing stock of the country and the I. and M. Executive will be many thousands out of pocket through paying compensation. I can save you all that worry.'

The Commissioner looked puzzled. 'That's all very well, A.Q.! You ask me not to make an arrest but you don't offer anything reasonable in exchange.

What's your theory?'

'As yet I haven't had time to form one, but I am convinced that no man would be such an idiot as to let the janitor see him arrive, go and deliberately kill Brunner with the proverbial blunt instrument, and then leave again as calmly as though going for a walk. No — it doesn't fit, man! Not in these days when a little ingenuity can scientifically eradicate a man from the face of the Earth . . . Give up the idea of arrest — at least for forty-eight hours. By then if I haven't produced something the field is yours.'

'And if Calhoun bolts?'

'If he does that will almost automatically point to his guilt — but I don't think he will. He's deeply attached to Monica Adley and for her sake I think he'll stay around.'

The Commissioner shrugged. 'Very well. I don't like doing it, but I can't help remember you are so often right . . . '

'I have never been wrong,' Quirke said simply, 'and I can't see why this occasion should be any exception.'

3

The Marks on the Mirror

When Quirke returned to his laboratory it was nearing noon, and he found Molly Brayson just at the close of her blood test. As Quirke entered she glanced up.

'It's Group AB, chief,' she announced. 'The rarest group of the lot — if that's any help.'

'Maybe: can't say at the moment.' The gigantic Quirke lumbered across to where she stood at the analysing bench. 'Nice work, light of my life. No wonder no man marries you. You'd probably know too much about him.'

The laboratory trembled and the man-mountain quaked and heaved volcanically; then the storm had passed again and Molly nodded towards Monica's overcoat.

'I've cleaned it as instructed, A.Q., but I am wondering what the police are going to say if they decide to analyse the bloodstain themselves.'

'They just can't, that's all. In any case I don't think they will trouble to do so: they're dead set on Calhoun because he was the only person to return to the observatory . . . Now pardon me a moment, light of my life. I must have a further word with the Commissioner.'

In another moment the Commissioner was on the line.

'What was Brunner's blood-group, Commissioner? Any idea?'

'Soon find out from Carter. Be in his record. Hang on . . . ' A long pause whilst Quirke puffed heavily and Molly cleared up the remains of her chemical activities; then, 'You there, A.Q.? Group AB. Does it signify?'

'It signifies this much: the blood on Monica Adley's sleeve was also AB. Molly's just checked on it. I know that AB isn't unique, that it isn't absolutely cast-iron in its certainty — but in a case like this we can't admit coincidence. The indications are that Monica got Brunner's blood on her coat sleeve. And you, I suppose, still think it doesn't matter?'

'Well . . . well, not at the moment. I'll table the information for future use — and thanks for telling me.'

'Don't mention it.' Quirke's voice was dry. 'I just love having my secretary work for the police when they should do it themselves.'

With that he rang off and frowned. Molly glanced at him and then came over.

'What's next, A.Q.? Or shall I deliver this coat to Miss Adley and get my own back?'

'One track mind,' Quirke muttered. 'They have themselves fixed on the obvious and won't turn from it — Consider this, light of my life: Monica Adley gets what I am convinced is Brunner's blood on her coat sleeve and yet doesn't go anywhere near him. Only looks at him! What's the answer to that?'

'We've only her word for it.'

'True, but — well, I don't think she's lying. Nor do I think she killed Brunner. But I *would* like to know where she got that stain from. Best thing we can do,

Molly, is go to the observatory and examine it for ourselves. Maybe the answer lies there. We'll stop for lunch somewhere on our way.'

★   ★   ★

It was two o'clock when Quirke brought his car to a halt outside the column's entrance hall. He and Molly alighted and for a moment they stood with their heads thrown back staring up at the fantastic rod which soared into apparent infinity and lost itself in the clouds.

'I have my doubts,' Quirke remarked, 'that this column is going to hold a weight like mine! However, hope for the best.'

He led the way into the entrance hall, nodded to the constable on guard duty, and so gained the elevator. Within a short time the observatory level had been gained and Joe sat watching as the girl and the gigantic scientist came into his line of vision.

'Mr. Quirke, isn't it?' The janitor got to his feet and gave a rather slovenly salute.

'So my fame spreads two miles up,'

Quirke exclaimed, beaming. 'And you will be Joe — janitor-cum-everything else?'

'That's right, Mr. Quirke — I'm Joe. I recognise you from your photograph in the papers now and again. 'ave the police sent you 'ere?'

Quirke winced. 'Hardly, dear man — hardly! I am a free agent in the matter and profoundly interested in Dr. Brunner's sudden and violent death. Later, doubtless, you will be of great help to me. For the moment I intend to examine the observatory.'

'Yes, sir. Up the steps there.'

Quirke looked at the ascent ladder to the upper floor and then sighed. Molly's slight smile did not improve things, either.

'All very well for you, m'girl, with your eight stone nothing,' he growled. 'I don't think the damned steps'll hold me!'

For once Quirke was wrong. The ladder was immensely strong and presently he had managed to heave his huge frame to the top and stumbled to the observatory floor. Here he stood wiping his face and chins with his sheet-like handkerchief whilst a nearby guardian constable touched his helmet. Quirke's vast size and mane of white hair were sufficient identification.

'Anything you'd like me to do, sir?' the constable asked, feeling it a novel sensation to be only as high as Quirke's ear.

'Yes,' Quirke admitted, 'but I don't think you'd do it!'

The laughter was overpowering and Quirke's face became dangerously red as he choked and spluttered over his hidden jest; then at last he calmed and found Molly dispassionately watching the globules of perspiration rolling down his face.

'Take it easy, boss, or one day you'll die laughing,' she warned. 'Now where do we start?'

'Hanged if I know. Usual routine — just looking to begin with.'

The constable watched with interest. Not that there was anything to observe, but he had heard tales of the genius of the eccentric Quirke. Certainly there was nothing impressive about wandering around the great observatory, peering at this and that . . . At the moment the roof hemispheres were closed and the steel plate had been put in position over the object glass.

Finally Quirke arrived at the mercuroid mirror — or at least the great carpet of silk-lined velvet that exactly covered it. Dubiously he looked at the chair on the observation arm, but thought better of climbing into it.

'May not take my weight,' he told Molly, as she looked at him questioningly.

'Take twenty like you, I bet! That girder's far stronger than you think, A.Q.'

'None the less I prefer to forego the exercise and the risk. You can take a ride instead and imagine you're a little girl again on a see-saw.'

'I can easily do that, but how does it help the Brunner case?'

'I want you to examine the chair carefully and see if there is any blood upon it.'

Molly nodded, climbed daintily to the narrow metal ledge along the arm edge, and then eased herself gradually into the softly sprung chair, a performance that the constable considered amply rewarding for hours of dull sentry duty.

Moments passed. Molly turned into various positions, examining the chair closely. Quirke puffed, perspired, and waited.

'Nothing,' Molly announced finally, and Quirke knew her well enough to know she had not skipped anything.

'Right,' he said. 'Just stay where you are, light of my life.'

He waddled across to the switch panel, surveyed it, then moved the control which started up the generator. Returning to the edge of the great covered mirror he said genially:

'Give yourself a ride, light of my life. I want to see what this chair arm can do when fully extended. The buttons are on the chair arms though, you'll have to work out for yourself which is which.'

Molly nodded once and, rather gingerly, tried the central green button. Immediately the chair got on the move, swirling back and forth across the mirror's cover like the pencil control on a giant telewriter. Molly did not look particularly happy as she was whisked back and forth but she clung on to the chair arms tenaciously and fiddled with the buttons. The result of this fiddling was that she suddenly stopped the chair's antics dead in its tracks and nearly plunged on to the covered mirror below.

'Mm . . . ' This from Adam Quirke, prolonged and pensive — at which Molly turned in the chair and gave him a chilly glance.

'You may see something amusing in these fairground antics, A.Q., but I don't! Anything more wanted?'

'Definitely there is, light of my life. Now you have the chair completely under control — or have you? — I want you to examine the side of the mirror wherever the chair arm is thrust out to its fullest extent. See if there are bloodstains.'

Molly muttered something but she did as instructed. By degrees, whilst Quirke watched intently, she manoeuvred the chair back and forth, examining the framework at the edge of the mirror carefully. At last she brought the chair to a standstill again.

'Nothing whatever, boss. Sorry.'

'No need to apologise, my dear: it isn't your fault. All right, you can now return to dry land.'

In a moment or two, still watched with interest by the constable, Molly had returned to safety. She straightened herself up a little and then gave her gigantic employer an enquiring glance.

'Where does all this get us?'

'I don't know about it getting us anywhere, but it does at least prove that when Brunner received that blow on the head he was not sitting in the reflector-chair, otherwise there would be blood-marks upon it, or if not there then on the edge of the mirror. Certainly there'd be some somewhere. Since there are not, we are led to the brilliant conclusion that Brunner was out of the chair when he was hit.'

'Sounds plausible,' Molly admitted.

'So now let us look further.' Quirke pulled away the silk-lined velvet covering and surveyed the highly polished surface from various angles.

'Beautiful stuff,' Molly murmured,

inspecting the silk-lined velvet. 'If you paid me more wages, A.Q., I could afford a dinner gown made of this stuff — '

'Take a look!' Quirke interrupted. 'That isn't a trick of the light, is it?'

She saw after a moment what he meant. By stooping and looking along the mirror from an oblique angle it was possible to observe slight flaws in its perfection, marks such as some sharp instrument might make.

'Recent or ancient?' Molly questioned, glancing.

'Recent, I think. The polisher for this mirror would otherwise have left traces in those minute cracks: instead, they catch and reflect the light. We make progress, light of my life: we make progress.'

Wheezing and coughing Quirke heaved himself forward so that he could lean over the mirror edge and inspect the scratches more closely through his pocket lens. He sweated and panted, turned nearly blue in the face, but finally succeeded in his object.

'Definitely new,' he announced, surging up again with Molly's assistance. 'No trace of the polisher having been near them, and since a mirror like this is polished daily with a special mechanism we can infer that these scratches were made last night.'

'By what?'

Quirke did not answer. After pondering for a moment he went over to the telephone shelf, studied the directory, and then dialled a number. Beaming on Molly, as she waited interestedly, he finally alerted as a voice came over the wire.

'Miss Adley? Good afternoon, my dear young lady. This is Adam Quirke. I'm speaking from the observatory. Now tell me something. Had Dr. Brunner any particular intention in mind when you left him last night? Astronomically, I mean.'

The girl's voice did not reach Molly but Quirke stood and listened intently.

'Betelgeuse, eh? Right, thank you very much — Pardon? No, I cannot give you any definite information yet. Yes. Good-bye.'

Quirke put the phone down and looked at Molly. She was obviously puzzled.

'So Brunner was studying Betelgeuse last night — or intended to. What about it?'

'Step by step I am finding my way,' Quirke responded, then all of a sudden his eyes vanished in layers of fat as he shook with silent merriment. 'About — about the last thing I'll ever do!' he spluttered at last. 'I can't even see my feet, never mind find my way step by step!'

Rumbling and exploding he dabbed at his eyes and then gradually began to quieten. Molly quietly led him back to the subject.

'Where's the connection between Brunner being flattened out and the fact that he meant studying Betelgeuse?'

'Just this. We can tell from the position the reflector would be in whilst he studied Betelgeuse, whether or not the mirror scratches might have been caused by his shoes.'

'Oh!' Molly did not look over-impressed. 'Surely he wouldn't be such an idiot as to walk on a mirror costing tens of thousands of pounds? Or whatever they do cost.'

Quirke did not answer this. Instead he rolled and lumbered to the nearest chair, sat down heavily, and then tugged out his pocketbook. For the next ten minutes he was absorbed in mathematics as he worked out the position Betelgeuse must have occupied in the sky the previous night, and the corresponding position of the reflector in order to be trained upon it.

'I think,' he said finally, 'the figures are clear enough. From them I can set the reflector in the position where it should have been in order to observe Betelgeuse whilst Earth turned on her axis. To work, light of my life — to work!'

Struggling to his feet he went across to the electrical equipment and spent another short interval determining the *modus operandi*. After which he experimented once or twice and was finally successful, starting up the generator and causing the reflector to turn when and where he wished. Ultimately he had the instrument pointed in what he believed was the correct position, and went across to it. Under the influence of the electric motor it was turning very gradually and counteracting Earth's revolution.

'Let it be truly said that Adam Quirke is all there,' he grinned, peering at the mirror. 'You observe the situation that now arises, light of my life?'

Not at all sure what was going on, Molly nevertheless gazed along the gleaming surface and then gave a little start of surprise.

'Why, the chair's movement would have to be limited within the area of the scratches if the reflector were not to be disturbed!'

'Precisely,' Quirke chuckled. 'The reflector is so poised, when on Betelgeuse, that only a fraction of the mirror is left clear, over which the telescopic chair could be projected. But if Brunner were to leave the chair suddenly he would contact the mirror at exactly the point where those scratches are!'

'But that only brings us back to where we were!' Molly protested. 'Why should he walk on the mirror itself instead of taking the normal path along the chair's supporting girder and so back to the observatory floor?'

'As to that . . . ' There was a faraway look in Quirke's china-blue eyes. 'As to that, Molly, we are compelled to believe in some urgent, impelling *necessity* for walking on the mirror. Something so insistent that Brunner simply had not the time to walk back the normal, slower way, but instead walked or ran along the mirror edge. What caused him to do that I'll be benighted if I know at this stage.'

'Couldn't have been because he'd been hit because there are no signs of bloodstains.'

'True.' Quirke reflected again and frowned to himself as he surveyed the immense mass of the reflector slowly moving on its gimbals.

'It seems,' Molly remarked, after a moment, 'that what we have to do is pin things down to one important question: What made Brunner move so suddenly he danced across the reflector glass?'

'Which is no easy job, my dear. Consider: he was presumably sitting in the telescopic chair, minding his own business and surveying Betelgeuse, then into this supposedly empty observatory there suddenly came something which made him move at top speed. I admit it has me stumped — for the moment.'

Quirke got on the move and surveyed the reflector again. It was only when he came to the base of it and the massive out-jutting bar by which, when necessary, it could be manhandled into a required position, that he suddenly stopped.

'The Fates are kind to their obese child,' he commented, and Molly moved quickly to his side.

'Found something?'

For answer Quirke motioned his hand, and even then Molly did not immediately realise what he meant. Then, going closer to the manual arm of the reflector she saw that its highly polished surface was defiled with dark smears. From a distance they looked exactly like wear, as though the plating had been worn from the arm by continual hand holding. But it was not that: it was a decided stain of some kind. Bloodstain?

'Do me a favour,' Quirke requested.

'Stand beside that manual arm, Molly, and let me look at you.'

Molly obeyed, accustomed to the most extraordinary instructions sometimes. Quirke surveyed her and nodded.

'Good! You and Monica Adley are of similar size and your coat sleeve comes on a line with that manual arm at almost the same point where Monica got blood on her sleeve. The inference, to quote my favourite, though old-fashioned, fictional detective, is obvious!'

'Meaning,' Molly said, turning to look at the manual arm, 'that this is a bloodstain and that it is where Monica received that smudge on her coat?'

'So it would appear. Monica said that she did not touch the body — that she merely looked. In the process of doing that, she could very easily have stood near this reflector and unwittingly got the stain on her sleeve. In fact,' Quirke continued, studying the dark marking on the polished metal, 'it is plain through this lens of mine that this stain is smeared through something brushing against it. Given sufficient magnification I daresay we'd discover some hairs from Monica's coat. We'd better look for ourselves when we get home. Get busy, my love, whilst I think further.'

Molly knew exactly what to do, and did it. Very carefully, using a stainless, steel-bladed penknife, she scraped the powdery brownness into a cellophane envelope and then put it away in her handbag.

'Do the police know about this, do you think?' she murmured, so her voice would not carry to the constable on duty.

'Probably. They don't miss much. They'll put their own construction on it if they do. The point that signifies is: what construction do we place on it? I'm surprised you haven't mentioned that,' Quirke finished, in a hurt voice.

Molly thought, and then started. 'Why, maybe that manual arm was used to hit Brunner with!'

Quirke chuckled and rumbled. 'Which means that the killer silently took the reflector from its gimbals and wielded it like a club, the manual arm happening to strike Brunner? Molly, my love, you can do better than that!'

'I know, but — I'd have to think about it, A.Q. Suppose, though, we're jumping to conclusions? This may not be Brunner's blood.'

'That's true, but I think it is. We'll know when we've made a laboratory test.' Quirke sat down heavily and mopped his face. 'Let us reflect, m'dear. If that blood is from Brunner, it means one of two things. One — he was seized by the throat and hammered against the manual arm, which points to somebody of quite considerable strength; or two: the reflector was swivelled around very rapidly and caught him a blow across the head. Which in turn does not explain the bruises on the throat . . . Mm, I don't like either conception very much.'

'Neither do I,' Molly admitted candidly. 'They don't explain away the scratches on the mirror, either.'

Quirke meditated through an interval, then nodded towards the bell-push. Molly went over and pressed it. As Quirke had expected, it presently brought the janitor into view.

'You want me, sir?' He looked at Quirke.

'I can assure you, Joe — which I understand to be your name — that I am not given to ringing bells for fun. Be so good as to come here a moment.'

'Aye, sir — that I will.'

Joe finished his ascent of the ladder and came over to where Quirke was seated.

'You were on duty here all last night, Joe?'

'I was, sir, yes. I am every night for that matter. Six months duty on, and six months off. Fair gets up me back sometimes, it does — '

'No doubt. I understand that Mr. Calhoun returned last night for some papers?'

''E did, sir, yes. And he went away with 'em. I saw 'im go.'

'How long did he take getting the papers?'

The Janitor pulled his ear and thought. 'Mebbe five or ten minnits. No more'n that.'

'And nobody else visited the observatory last night?'

'Not a soul, sir. There was only me and Dr. Brunner 'ere. I don't know what 'e was doin'. I could 'ear 'im movin' about at times. It was around three o'clock and I'd gone to bed — as I'm entitled to do — when I 'eard Dr. Brunner give an awful cry. Fair froze me blood, it did.'

'After which you investigated?'

'I did that — yes. I found — '

'We know what you found, Joe. Tell me this: how did the observatory look? What details can you remember?'

'Looked to me just the same as it's ever done. The roof was wide open and the gale was just starting to blow real 'ard. Rain was startin', too. The reflector was pointed skywards, but I wouldn't know what at. Seemed kind of silly to me to 'ave it in action with the storm getting up — '

'The storm arrived suddenly,' Quirke put in. 'I know that from personal observation. It followed a night of unusual calm and clearness. Right! So the roof was open and the reflector in position for making some observation or other. Brunner lay on the floor.'

'That's it, sir.'

'And there was no trace of anybody else present and Calhoun had long since gone?'

The janitor nodded. Quirke sat hunched forward, his brows knitted as he strove to see light in the darkness. Finally he gave a sigh and relaxed a trifle. His sharp eyes moved back to the janitor.

'You didn't particularly like Dr. Brunner, did you?'

The janitor shrugged. 'Nobody did for that matter. 'E was a queer 'un. Liked the ladies, too.'

'I mean,' Quirke continued, 'that you had a particular grudge against him because he was going to make things unpleasant for you over that pet gossamer-spider of yours.'

'Aye, but — You don't suppose I'd try and get even with 'im by murderin' 'im, do you?'

Quirke grinned disarmingly. 'Frankly, no . . . And where is your extraordinary pet at the moment?'

'In 'is corner down below as usual. Been off somewhere durin' the night though — just like a blinkin' cat. Always on the wander. I noticed before I 'ad me breakfast that he wasn't about: then about arf an hour later he turned up again.'

'From where?'

'I dunno. I just 'appened to notice 'e'd come back. 'e wanders anywhere around and spins 'is blinkin' webs. That was what Dr. Brunner objected to: didn't like a spider in the observatory though I can't think why it mattered.'

'Well, Joe, thank you for being so explicit,' Quirke said, heaving to his feet. 'You can go back to your quarters.'

'Aye, sir. Whenever you want me you can always find me there.'

Quirke watched him go and then turned to Molly. 'I think we have done all we can here, light of my life. Let's be on our way.'

The girl nodded and led the way to the descent ladder. Quirke, after a final glance around and a nod to the constable, followed her, but he did not immediately head for the elevator. Instead he paused in the janitor's quarters immediately below the observatory and surveyed the layout. Not that there was anything unusual. There was a table couple of chairs, an easy, a radio-televisor, bookshelf — all the necessities of a man forced to live in one particular spot for half a year at a time. Joe himself made no effort to prevent Quirke's inspection: he was busy at the small sink apparently washing up the few crocks from his breakfast.

'And this is your little friend, eh?' Quirke enquired, gazing at a corner of the ceiling where the magnificent, rainbow-hued insect was apparently asleep amidst its fabric-like web.

'Aye, that's Loony,' Joe confirmed.

'You should have been named Bruce, my friend,' Quirke commented solemnly; then he burst into laughter at the janitor's vacant stare. 'No matter — just a joke.'

Gurgling to himself and his eyes out of sight, Quirke lumbered into the corridor and across to the elevator where Molly was awaiting him. She realised from the pink face and little tears of merriment that some preposterous joke or other had been exploded.

'Are we ready to go?' she asked, and Quirke nodded.

'Quite ready. I have just been making the acquaintance of Loony, the Martian gossamer-spider. Interesting insects. I shall feel that my education has been badly neglected until I have learned more about them.'

Molly pressed the button that opened the gates and she and Quirke stepped into the elevator. After they had reached the ground floor it was only a short while before they were back in the laboratory and Molly's first duty — as was usual about this time — was to prepare cups of tea for herself and her employer. Meanwhile he contacted the Metropolitan Weather Bureau and spoke to the Chief Meteorologist.

'I want an exact report on last night's weather over London,' Quirke explained. 'I'll have the recorder take it down as you give it.'

'Pleasure, Mr. Quirke. One moment . . . ' Then after only a brief pause the meteorologist's voice resumed and Quirke listened whilst he watched the slowly revolving spools of the recording equipment linked to the telephone.

'Weather report as from midnight last night. Calm with wind falling light southerly until two-fifty a.m. At that time the encroachment of a secondary brought a sudden change in wind direction and marked increase in velocity, together with rain. By three-thirty a.m. a full gale was recorded, with heavy rain. Later it — '

'Later doesn't signify, thank you,' Quirke interrupted. 'Was the sky clear between midnight and three a.m.?'

'Yes, quite clear. Wind velocity then was only about sixteen miles an hour.'

'Thank you; that's fine.'

With that, Quirke rang off, the report quite clear in his mind without him having to refer to the recorded version of it. He took the cup of tea Molly offered him and she looked at him questioningly.

'Does the weather report fit into things, boss?'

'It might. I was just satisfying myself upon what I already remembered about it — namely that nobody with a helicopter or other flying device would venture out knowing the kind of weather which was forecast. That angle can be safely rubbed out, I imagine.'

'We seem to be getting nowhere fast, A.Q.'

'I wouldn't say that,' Quirke mused, stirring his tea. 'All these odd bits and pieces fit in the jig-saw somewhere. One thing we do know: terror was the main accompaniment of Brunner's death. First he ran along the mirror, and second he gave a blood-curdling scream, according to the janitor.'

'You believe what the janitor said, then?'

'I do, yes, chiefly because I don't see why he should need to lie over a matter like that. Now, what else have we got? Calhoun was only five to ten minutes in the room adjoining the janitor's quarters, getting his missing papers. Had he gone up to the observatory proper he would have had to ascend the ladder outside the janitor's quarters and thereby been seen. Had he done so the janitor would certainly have mentioned it — if only to protect himself against suspicion. On the other hand I don't think Calhoun would have been crazy enough to take such a risk knowing the janitor was able to observe him.'

'There is, of course, one other fantastic possibility,' Molly said, her gaze turned inward in speculation. 'It is that Calhoun returned when he knew the janitor had gone to bed — for he must have had a reasonably good idea of the hours he keeps — and silently went up to the observatory, knowing beforehand probably that Brunner was going to be on a late session studying Betelgeuse. He killed him somehow, probably by seizing him by the throat and banging his head on the manual arm of the reflector, then he got away again before the janitor investigated.'

Quirke sighed. 'Then why did Brunner leave the reflector chair so quickly, so agitatedly indeed, that he crossed the mirror? Seeing Calhoun wouldn't have scared him, particularly as he would have no idea of Calhoun's intentions.'

'Maybe Calhoun dragged him out of

the chair and his heels slid along the mirror?'

'And maybe not, light of my life! As for your conception that Calhoun made good his escape before the janitor investigated — no, it positively won't do! The moment he heard that cry the janitor was on the move. You weigh up the size of that observatory, the distance Calhoun would have to go from the reflector, then descend the ladder, and *then* use the elevator, the motor of which whines all the time the elevator is in action . . . It does not fit.'

'Then suppose Calhoun had a rope with him and hung himself outside the observatory dome until he was reasonably sure the janitor had finished prowling?'

'How, then, did the janitor get Calhoun at his apartment when he almost immediately rang him?'

'I'd overlooked that,' Molly admitted, crestfallen. 'Let's try something else, then How much do we know of Sasmo of Procyon? What particular powers has he that we of Earth have not? Suppose he is able to walk through walls, suspend himself in mid-air against the law of gravity, or even rotate himself into the fourth dimension?'

Quirke shrugged. 'Perhaps he can do all or any of these things: I wouldn't know, and it's certain he'd never reveal the fact if he possesses such useful gifts. But against that, why should a being having such supernormal power be content with a common or garden way of murdering Brunner? The two don't balance. From Sasmo one would expect a skilful, extremely complex way of eliminating Brunner, and one without any guilt attaching to himself.'

'Unless Sasmo has deliberately been 'ordinary' to throw the police off the scent.'

Quirke considered this for a moment or two, then he shook his head and set down his empty cup.

'Sorry, Molly, it doesn't ring a bell anywhere. We're way off the beam somewhere and the sooner we get back on it the better. Let me have those scrapings from the manual arm, will you?'

Molly brought the cellophane envelope

from her overcoat and thereafter Quirk went to work. His first move was to subject the scrapings to careful study under the electron microscope, and here indeed certain obvious facts became revealed. For one thing, the dark scrapings were dried blood, and for another there were numerous short lengths of what appeared to be rope when under the electron microscope but which were actually hairs from Monica Adley's coat. That they exactly matched hairs from the coat itself — still in Quirke's possession — was in itself conclusive.

And even more interesting was the analysis of the dried blood itself. It was Group AB once again.

4

Molly in Peril

'From this,' Molly remarked, when the analysis was complete, 'it would appear that we can rule out Monica henceforth — at least as far as guilt through bloodstained coat is concerned. Why not tell the Commissioner and give him a shock?'

Quirke grinned. 'That's an idea . . . '

He crossed to the telephone and at length the Commissioner's voice came through. He listened without interruption to the story Quirke gave him.

'Very interesting,' he said finally. 'The pity is that you haven't been very original, Quirke. We noticed the stain on the manual arm and had it analysed. You can't prove that Monica Adley stood in such a position as to get the stain on her sleeve so I don't see it in any way lessens guilt against her.'

'You wouldn't,' Quirke snorted. 'Whilst we're about it, how do you suppose Brunner was knocked out with the manual arm? It isn't detachable from the reflector, remember, so that it might be used as a weapon.'

'Our guess is that the killer seized Brunner by the throat and banged his head against the manual arm.'

'I see. In that case he would have had to be attacked from the back in order to bang his head on the front. Yet the position of the stranglehold marks are plainly those of somebody holding the throat from the front. How about that?'

'That,' the Commissioner answered evasively, 'is one of the things we haven't yet reconciled.'

'Not the only thing either, I'll gamble. All right, since I can't convince you that I don't think Monica Adley should any longer come under suspicion, I'll ring off — '

'Before you do, Quirke, how long are you going to be offering something tangible? I can't hold off for ever in making an arrest, you know!'

'For ever! Good Lord, man, I only started this morning. I'm not a magician, remember!'

'Sometimes I've even wondered about that,' the Commissioner murmured grudgingly, and then Quirke grinned and put down the telephone. Molly, who had overheard the other end of the conversation, gave a sigh.

'Apparently they're level with us, boss. They've seen everything we've seen.'

'Except the solution,' Quirke responded, and broke into a hurricane of merriment that ended with him flopping into a chair and gasping for breath.

'About this coat,' Molly said, picking it up. 'Shall I let Monica have it back?'

Quirke hardly seemed to hear her. Having recovered from his mirthful hysteria he was gazing before him thoughtfully.

'I don't think they are level with us,' he said. 'Nowhere has the Commissioner mentioned scratches on the reflector mirror. That would probably escape the men of the law since it is more a specialist's job to weigh up a telescopic mirror. In that there perhaps lies a lead, though heaven forbid that this investigation should descend into a vulgar rivalry to see who can find the answer first. Let's see now. To our own satisfaction, Molly, we have eliminated Monica and Calhoun. That leaves the murky Sasmo and the janitor. Mm, the *janitor* . . . '

Quirke screwed up his eyes and fondled his fleshy chins.

'You said you think he's innocent,' Molly remarked.

'I did, and I do. Chiefly because he's too obvious a culprit by being the only other person present with Brunner. There is also the theory that he is too old to attack a man of Brunner's strength. No. I think he can be eliminated. That leaves us with Sasmo, and all the information we'll get out of that inscrutable alien won't get us very far. We have to assess what opportunity he had, and unless he does possess powers such as those suggested by you, my love, I don't think he had any opportunity at all. Also I believe, as aforesaid, that he'd be cunningly scientific about a murder and not rely on the normal way of eliminating his victim.'

'Which means you've disposed of all the suspects,' Molly pointed out. 'We've nothing left to work on.'

'Don't be too sure of that, m'dear!' Quirke heaved out of his chair, and began to pace up and down slowly, filling his worn briar pipe meanwhile. 'We have that matter of scratches on the mirror and the unearthly scream to dwell upon. What *could* it have been which so terrified Brunner?'

'I wonder,' Molly said slowly, 'if it was a cry of terror or a cry of *pain*? Not very easy to tell the difference.'

Quirke swung, his china-blue eyes bright. 'For that unexpected slice of wisdom, my love, I could kiss you — only I'm afraid of the wife!'

With an effort Quirke subdued an upboiling of merriment and lighted his pipe.

'A cry of *pain*! Ah, now it actually looks as though it might fit into the picture. Did the cry come after or *before* the scratches on the mirror? It would help us a deal if we knew, but unfortunately we never shall. Did Brunner perhaps see something in the reflector mirror which frightened the wits out of him and he made a dash away from whatever it was?'

'Can't think why he should,' Molly said, frowning. 'It seems pretty conclusive that he was studying Betelgeuse, and there's nothing peculiar about that star.'

'True enough — the ruddy star in the constellation of Orion. No, nothing unusual about that. Let us consider again: did Brunner meet his death *not* through human agency after all but because of something he saw, or sensed, or viewed through the reflector?'

'That spoils everything, boss! What about the blow on the head and the marks of strangulation on the throat?'

Quirke thought. 'There's an answer to everything,' he said finally, 'and perhaps the blow on the head and the throat marks will slide into place of themselves as we get further on. The fact remains that from here on I shall work from the angle that human beings — or a human being — did not cause Brunner's death, but something else. Terrifying, unique, maybe never heard of before —

'Tonight,' Quirke finished, 'we shall return to the observatory and, weather permitting, will spend some time observing Betelgeuse and see if it tells us anything . . . '

'Right,' Molly confirmed. Since she had no home ties and no boyfriend it wouldn't matter if she spent all night on the job — and she probably would.

'We'll need a strong crane or derrick,' Quirke added solemnly, but there were twinkling lights in his eyes.

'We will?' Molly sensed that humour, elephantine and obscure, was about to well forth.

'Certainly! If I should see something in that mirror that flattens me out, how will a slim youngster like you be able to haul me to a sofa or something? Definitely we'll need a crane!'

The storm broke and finished with Quirke having nearly laughed himself into a stupor. Molly looked at him in concern.

'That isn't funny in any language, boss. If there's a real danger of your being killed then don't experiment. Have the

Commissioner try it instead.'

Which only started Quirke off again. He whipped out his vast handkerchief and wept into it, then as his merriment dropped to gale force he managed to get out words again.

'I'm only joking, light of my life. I don't think for a moment we — or I — will see anything horrible in the mirror, but since the reflector has not been tampered with since Brunner died we might be able to see what he saw, and thereby take a giant stride towards the very elusive solution.'

'Could be,' Molly admitted, then she picked up Monica's coat and tossed it over her arm. 'I'll nip off home for a while, boss, and freshen up, leaving this with Monica on the way. What time do you want me back here?'

'Oh, around eight o'clock should be soon enough,' Quirke told her. 'Fortunately the wife won't be back until late tonight so I shall not have to inflict my fascinating company upon her. Being all alone I think I might turn the time to good advantage by reading up on gossamer-spiders and their habits.'

On that Molly took her departure and, true to his decision, Quirke selected the most informative book he could find in his library, concerning the insect-life of Mars, and then settled down to read. He started slightly when interruption came at last in the bosomy form of the house-keeper.

'Begging your pardon, sir, but what time will madam be back? Shall I prepare dinner as usual?'

'No, Mrs. Whittaker, thanks. I am going out, and Mrs. Quirke's time of return is doubtful . . . What time is it?'

'Why, it's — ' Mrs. Whittaker glanced towards the mantelshelf. 'Seven o'clock, sir.'

'Dear me!' Quirke laid the book aside and gave a fatuous grin. 'Shows how absorbed you can get. Know anything about gossamer-spiders, Mrs. Whittaker?'

'Good Lord, no, sir, and I don't want to! I don't know what things are coming to these days with these importations from another planet! Didn't happen in my young days.'

Quirke grinned as the housekeeper left

the library and closed the door; then he sat thinking for a while.

'Interesting little devils,' he muttered. 'Very interesting. I must bounce my knowledge against the delectable Molly and see what she thinks about it.'

With a good deal of asthmatic wheezing he fought his way to his feet and spent half an hour freshening up for the evening's work. Instead of the normal dinner he satisfied himself with a couple of concentrates from the laboratory — and by this time Molly was due.

As usual she was punctual, entering the laboratory at exactly eight o'clock to find Quirke in his huge overcoat and his mane of white hair more untidy than ever.

'Anything new, boss?' Molly asked brightly.

'Depends,' Quirke answered thoughtfully. 'I have been studying the habits of the gossamer-spider — a most interesting occupation. Were you aware that, unlike the Earth spider, the Martian one does not spin a web in order to catch its victims, it does it because it *has* to.'

'Has to? In what way?'

'Well, just as we human beings automatically eliminate waste products from our systems in order to live and stay healthy, so the Martian spider excretes its web in order to keep normal. Just another of those complex elimination systems devised by bountiful Mother Nature.'

Molly did not look particularly interested; nor was she.

'Further,' Quirke continued, 'the gossamer-spider is instantly attracted towards anything polished and gleaming, but not necessarily a bright light, as is our Earth moth . . . There are a host of things about the Martian spider that are most instructive. Not that I have found any connection yet which might help us along with the problem on hand, but I'm still hoping . . . However, we must be on our way. I gather the night is clear and serene outside.'

'Couldn't be better for astronomical observation,' Molly agreed, opening the laboratory's outer door and stepping outside.

'Did Monica Adley have anything to say when you returned the coat?'

'Nothing of importance, but she seemed pretty glad that you had decided against her being the killer. I didn't step out of line by telling her that, did I?'

'Not at all, light of my life. Better the lady knows that somebody is on her side.'

Quirke opened the car door and Molly slid into the seat next to the steering wheel. In a matter of moments Quirke had the car on its way and before long the mighty observatory column came into view in the pale western afterglow. By the time the top of the column had been reached almost complete darkness had settled.

As usual, the janitor emerged to investigate. In his quarters, seated eating a meal, was the night-duty constable. He got to his feet and saluted as he beheld Quirke's mighty figure in the corridor.

'Just having a snack, Mr. Quirke, before I go on a night's duty,' he explained. 'The chief wouldn't like me taking things this easy, I'm afraid, so would you — '

'My dear man, your guilty secret is safe with me,' Quirke grinned. 'Even policemen must live — though heaven knows why!'

With that, chuckling convulsively, Quirke began to heave himself up the ladder into the observatory proper, Molly climbing up behind him. The constable and janitor watched them ascend, then evidently with the realisation that he could not recline and eat indefinitely the constable hurried above.

'Anything I can do, sir?' he asked eagerly, and Quirke turned from a study of the reflector to look at him.

'Yes — keep quiet and leave us alone.'

The constable muttered something and turned away. Quirke rid himself of his overcoat and then went across to the control panel. In a moment or two the roof hemispheres had slid back and the motor controlling the movement of the reflector had started up.

'Inclination nine, boss,' Molly said, looking up from the abstruse mathematics she had been working out. 'Degree sixteen, and lateral four. That aught to put you in line with Betelgeuse. That is if Mr. Brunner's own figuring here on the approximate position of the star is correct.'

'It will be,' Quirke assured her. 'Brunner was not the kind of man to misfire on his maths.' He lumbered forward and then pulled away the silk-velvet cover of the mirror. This done he carefully edged his ponderous bulk on to the girder supporting the telescopic chair. Nothing gave way, even as Molly had said it wouldn't in the first instance. So Quirke kept on going until at last he had reached the chair and sank gingerly into it. 'So far, so good,' he commented, beaming upon Molly as she watched from the side of the mirror. 'Now, let us see how our old friend Betelgeuse looks — and if anything queer happens just brace yourself. In that way we may discover the answer we're looking for.'

Molly gave a nod and Quirke moved the switch which brought the mighty reflector into action immediately there appeared on the mirror the blazing majesty of the constellation of Orion. Observation could not have been clearer, with Betelgeuse itself a shimmering ruby blaze in the midst of it.

'Very nice,' Qnirke commented, steering the chair over the mirror to improve the viewing angle. 'How does it strike you, light of my life?'

Molly was now standing on the mirror's metal rim, gazing down at the reflected stars at her feet. The huge mirror looked to her exactly like a lake, or else a great abyss in the Earth through which she was looking at the sky beyond.

'Wonderful!' she whispered. 'Absolutely wonderful! The stars look just like jewels, A.Q.'

Quirke sighed. 'Damn me, are all you women alike? Everything has to be relegated to jewels, or money, or velvet, or something! Concentrate, girl! These are stars you are looking at. Do you see anything unusual about Betelgeuse?'

'The one like a ruby? No — it looks all right to me. But don't forget I've never had a look through a telescope as big as this before so I'm no judge. What exactly did you expect?'

'I don't really know.' Quirke sounded genuinely disappointed. 'Somehow I had half expected something terrifying, some-thing to account for Brunner's obvious fright. As it is . . . I might try the finer focus and see if it helps any.'

Reaching to the control buttons on the chair, Quirke selected one and pressed it. Immediately Betelgeuse alone seemed to fill most of the mirror a hazy and pulsating red cauldron, its edge furred with distance and atmospheric vibration.

'Nice, but it still doesn't tell us anything,' Quirke remarked. 'Switch off the lights, Molly, and see if it's any different that way.'

Molly obeyed, but the descent of darkness on the observatory — except for starshine from the heavens above — only served to make Betelgeuse and its neighbours clearer on the mirror. Most certainly there was no sign of anything unusual.

'All right,' Quirke sighed. 'Lights up again.'

In the return of the effulgence he sat thinking, hunched forward like a white-haired Buddha in the telescopic chair. Molly returned to the edge of the mirror and looked at him enquiringly.

'Can a puzzled little girl ask what you're getting at, A.Q.? How did you expect Betelgeuse to react? It's only a normal star after all, isn't it?'

'True.' Quirke glanced across at her moodily. 'I just hoped we might find something unusual about it — something to make us terrified, even maybe an unusual aberration of light waves which might have affected Brunner's brain in some strange way . . . But there it is! Everything just perfect. Too perfect.'

Molly became silent, waiting. At length Quirke struggled out of the chair and made his way back along the girder. When he reached the floor he stood with his head thrown back gazing up at the massive length of the reflector.

'I think,' he said finally, 'I'll take a look at the object glass on that thing. Might be interesting. You stay here and angle the instrument about until the top is level with that outer parapet.'

'Okay,' Molly assented, and Quirke turned to the ladder that led to the steel lip of the roof slot above. After five minutes of dragging his immense weight upward he reached the narrow, railed space beyond and for a moment or two stood gazing down on the patchwork of lights two miles below.

'Ready, boss?' Molly's voice came floating up from below, and Quirke gave a start.

'Yes, yes, light of my life! Swing the big fellow round!'

Immediately the huge reflector started moving and after a good deal of trial and error, for she was by no means used to handling the equipment, Molly had the instrument at such an angle that its object glass was dead level with the parapet. Here she locked the gimbal system and watched Quirke as he inspected the mighty lens with his pocket torch. At the end of nearly ten minutes close scrutiny he withdrew and shook his head as he looked down on Molly.

'No use, light of my life. Nothing unusual, once again ... Restore the reflector to its normal angle and then come up here and join me.'

Molly did as she was told. At the far

end of the observatory the guardian constable had arrived at the conclusion that the giant with the white hair was crazy and the girl in slacks and overcoat not far short of it. With the police entirely satisfied as to the culprit where was the need for all this monkeying about? Which probably explained why the constable was still a constable and had not done anything yet worthy of promotion.

'Well, A.Q., what are we looking for?' Molly asked brightly, coming up to Quirke's side.

'Anything we can find. Let us make sure — absolutely sure — that nothing came from up here to attack Brunner. If anything did there'll be traces. A scratch on the metal here and there, maybe a scrap of mud or dirt — though I fancy the rain would wash that away last night. We'll hang on to *anything*, m'dear. Let's take a look. You go left and I'll go right.'

They did, and spent fifteen minutes making a slow circuit of the opened roof, but not a worthwhile thing did they find. At length they met again at the point where they had first started.

'Pity,' Quirke sighed. 'Great pity.'

'Suppose,' Molly said, 'that we cast back a moment to my suggestion that maybe Calhoun returned later. If he wiped out Brunner and then escaped over the parapet here, he could have been wearing rubber soled shoes that wouldn't leave any sign of scratching. He could also,' Molly continued in triumph, 'perhaps lower himself by a doubled rope — so it could be withdrawn when he'd finished the descent — down to the half-way point of the column. You know where I mean — the spot where the metal expands and contracts in the wind. After that, if he didn't use the elevator because of the noise the control motor would make, he could go down the stairway to the ground. A long way to descend, certainly — nearly a mile — but he could do it. Then away — and off home.'

'Apparently,' Quirke said, 'you have been doing quite a lot of thinking, m'dear, to trot out such an elaborated version of your original hypothesis.'

'My job is to think further,' Molly explained modestly. 'I can sometimes fill in the blanks which the great man misses.'

'That being so,' Quirke said pleasantly, 'we have no other course than to put the idea to the test and time it. If it could be done in a certain time then we shall consider it carefully.'

'Meaning what?' Molly's bright face was uneasy in the light reflecting from below.

'Meaning, my dear, that you will be Calhoun.'

'Oh!' Molly looked over the parapet into the yawning void with the infinitesimal lights below. Then she glanced back to Quirke. 'We haven't got a rope that long.'

'According to your theory Calhoun must have had one, therefore so must we. I would suggest the triple-X steel wire which is so extensively used these days.'

'But — but, boss, you don't expect me to go overboard, do you? I mean — I daren't! I mean, I can't!'

'Which makes you a coward when you have to prove your own theory? Shame on thee, lass!'

'It isn't that. It's different for a man.'

'Why is it? You're young and agile, and this is a matter which demands proof if it is to be accepted . . . ' Quirke turned and looked into the lighted observatory. 'Constable!'

'Yessir . . . ' The constable came quickly into view.

'Fetch a drum of triple-X steel wire from somewhere even if you have to go back to headquarters to do it! I'll take the responsibility. Length of the wire must be about two miles.'

'Yessir. Immediately.'

'I think it's a dirty trick, A.Q.,' Molly grumbled. 'You know I'm not cut out for this sort of thing — '

'I don't know anything of the kind. I feel that you have put forward a theory which *might* be possible, and we cannot afford to ignore any lead. I don't feel up to trusting myself with a triple-X wire with my bulk, but you can do it well enough. From the moment you start off to the time you reach the ground I'll time you. When you've got to the ground phone me up here.'

'All right,' Molly sighed and bowed to

the inevitable. Then she pulled off her overcoat and tucked her blouse more tightly in the top of her slacks. Quirke surveyed her young, lithe form enviously.

'What it is to be a child,' he sighed.

'*Who's* a child? Look here, boss, I — '

'To me, light of my life, you'll always be a child, both physically and mentally. Incidentally, if our friend used a double wire, as you suggest, there'd be scored marks around one or other of these railings supports at floor level. I haven't seen any.'

'Probably my theory's dead wrong then,' Molly said promptly.

'I don't think so. Calhoun — or indeed Sasmo or Monica — could have prepared for the attack any time they wished. They could have smuggled a two-mile length of silk rope up here and hidden it. That would leave no traces at all on metal.'

'If Calhoun didn't perform this gymnastic feat then Sasmo might have done,' Molly said, musing. 'He looks the tough, iron nerved type who'd never bat an eyelash at a stunt like this.

'And Monica isn't the fainting type

either,' Quirke added.

Molly gave it up. She had made ineffectual wriggles to get out of this assignment, but evidently Quirke was not having any. Finally she sat down on the roof ledge and tossed her coat about her shoulders as protection against the cool night wind. Quirke meanwhile surveyed the dark immensity below, his thoughts busy but none of them conclusive. Finally he looked up towards the brightly clear constellation of Orion and the twinkling Betelgeuse. Something from outer space perhaps, which had scared Brunner immeasurably? Something that would never be repeated?

'I got it, Mr. Quirke!'

Quirke stirred and Molly made a sound suspiciously like a groan. The constable was below, cradling in his arm one of the larger drums of extremely thin yet incredibly tough wire used almost universally these days for engineering and other jobs demanding the maximum of strength with the minimum of bulk.

'Thank you constable. Throw it up . . .'

The constable obeyed and Quirke deftly caught the drum as it came sailing towards him. Molly struggled to her feet and made a wry face as she tossed aside her overcoat.

'All yours, m'dear,' Quirke said cheerfully.

'Fat lot you care if I break my neck, A.Q.!

'You won't do that, m'dear, or I wouldn't let you attempt the feat. You'll be all right, and you may even prove your theory is possible. Heaven knows, we can do with something concrete.'

Molly took the drum and began to play the wire out into the void below. When it reached the halfway mark on the wire, revealed by a white mark dyed in the wire itself, she passed the wire once round one of the rail supports and then tossed the drum into the abyss. Which meant that the wire was now a mile long, doubled.

'Ready?' Quirke asked her at length.

'Yes, you inquisitor of innocent young women!'

'Right.' Quirke took out his watch and studied the flicking second hand. 'You have just killed Brunner and have got to this ledge and played out the wire. That job took in all approximately seven minutes. Now, you are making good your escape — One, two, three — go!'

Molly did not hesitate any longer. Quickly she threw her legs over the rail, caught hold of the doubled wire, and then began to descend into the gulf, her knees scissored round the wire and her handkerchief between her palms to save them being blistered. Down she went, as fast as she dared, and the vast high-flung bulk of the column summit with the reflected light of the observatory dome began to recede against the stars. It was a dizzying, nightmare drop, but Molly kept her nerve. As she dropped she checked herself ever and again as she felt the heat of friction searing through her handkerchief and through her slacks.

Then down again. Here and there she risked glancing below to see whether she had reached the halfway point of the column, but it was not a feat she cared to repeat too often. Hanging on that length of wire the ground nearly a mile and a half below was more than a dizzying task unless she kept her gaze either level or above.

Then suddenly the unexpected — and it was nearly at what she judged was the end of her drop. The handkerchief smouldered away in her hands and the sudden pain of burning friction across her palms made her gasp in anguish. She released one hand in sheer pain and swung on with the other. She dropped several feet and felt as if her remaining clinging hand had been seared down to the bones.

'A.Q.!' she screamed. 'I can't hold on! I've burned myself — !'

He probably did not hear her. She jammed her knees tightly together and stopped her descent at the expense of skinned legs. But her hands were useless, blistered and smarting. With a dizzying effort she swung her shoulders outwards so that the wire wrapped diagonally about her waist. For the rest she hooked the insides of her elbows about the wire and there hung precariously, trying to imagine how she should act next.

The trouble was that since the observatory ledge projected some eight feet beyond the column itself, it was not possible for her to brace against the column without swinging herself forward, and with her hands so ragged and burned she just could not dare to grip with them. Only the knee grip and the diagonal pull across her waist was preventing her dropping to the end of the wire, and after that —

'Boss!' she screamed again. 'I'm stuck! I daren't move! Pull me up!'

On the ledge far above Quirke did not hear a word. The wind blew Molly's words away. And yet, as she hung listening desperately, she heard a reply. But it was not Quirke. It was a quiet, unnaturally perfect intonation.

'Make an effort to swing to the column, young lady. I will do the rest.'

Molly got the impression that she was probably dreaming since there just couldn't be anybody at this fantastic height up the column. Nevertheless, if it meant a chance of salvation it was worth trying. So she began swinging slowly, finally achieving enough impetus to actually touch the column's side. Instantly a firm hand gripped her ankles and stopped her swinging outwards again.

'Let yourself go,' the voice instructed. 'I have you firmly enough.'

Molly obeyed, reasonably certain she was going to drop to her death. She unhooked her half paralysed arms from the wire and twisted her shoulders. Instantly she was free — but she did not drop. It seemed to her that one hand only remained about her ankles whilst the other caught her at the back of the neck. She was impelled inwards, roughly at first, then more gently, and carefully laid upon her back. She felt metal through her blouse but for the moment was too faint to understand what was happening.

Then slowly she realised that she had actually reached the halfway point of the column and was lying on the narrow metal platform in which lay the trapdoor to the down-stretch stairway. And her rescuer? He loomed against the stars — square, thick-legged, wide-shouldered . . .

'Who — who are you?' Molly whispered, rising on to one elbow.

There was no hesitation over the answer. 'Sasmo of Procyon.'

5

Quirke Examines a Corpse

For a long moment Molly just could not take the situation in at all. Sasmo of Procyon? Here? Halfway up the column and conveniently in time to save her from certain death? Indeed, from what she knew of him — which was little — the surprising thing was that he had even taken the trouble to save her.

'I gather,' his quiet, cynical voice remarked, 'that you were in difficulties, young woman? Who are you and what were you doing?'

'My name's Molly Brayson. As to what I was doing . . . Well, never mind. I was making an experiment.'

'Apparently a dangerous one. Swinging on a wire a mile above ground is not a good idea unless you're trained to it. Molly Brayson, you said? Assistant to Adam Quirke, the scientific detective?'

'Yes.' Molly pinned her anguishing hands between her arms and her body and gritted her teeth. 'Now you know that, I suppose you feel like kicking me into the depths?'

'I have no such intention. It would seem more expedient to get you medical aid immediately. I gather your hands are paining you considerably. Since I am ascending the column you had better come with me. If you are not able to walk — or rather climb — you can trust yourself to me.'

Molly did not say anything. She was confused, both with the situation and the pain in her hands. The column was so devised that the upper half had no means whatever of communicating with the summit, except by helicopter. This had been done to prevent possible saboteurs from below trying to wreck the costly astronomical equipment, whilst the lower half was provided with an internal ladder so that constant supervision could be maintained over the contracting and expanding section upon which the column's security depended.

'Did you say — climb?' Molly asked at last.

'I did. I had intended to make the ascent alone, of course, but your extra weight will not incommode me in any way. I have strength which you of Earth would consider supernormal, but that is purely the outcome of the high-gravity planet from which my ancestors came.'

Again Molly was silent. The first question that leapt to her mind was to ask why Sasmo was behaving as he was and what he was doing here. Then she decided that perhaps the questions were better left to Adam Quirke.

'You mean climb up the outside of the column?' she asked abruptly.

'Naturally. From this halfway point there is no way up the interior of the column: I have already made sure of that. But there are sufficient projections and metal brackets on the outside of the structure to provide ample foot and handhold. Do you care to trust yourself to me?'

Molly looked at the solidly-built, round-headed figure against the stars,

134

then whatever hesitation she had vanished as her burned hands gave an extra vicious twinge.

'All right,' she said quietly. 'I don't know how you propose to carry me. I can't possibly hold on to you with my hands.'

'You can with your arms locked under my chin.' Sasmo went down on hands and knees. 'Sit astride my back and put your arms under my chin. That way your hands will not be needed.'

Molly got to her feet and obeyed the instructions. This was nothing more than the piggy-back of her childhood days. When at length she was fairly comfortably settled, the man from Procyon got to his feet and Molly could not help noticing that her weight seemed to make no difference to him. He moved with strong, sure strides to the edge of the platform, reached up to the first projections, and then began to climb.

Molly shut her eyes and hoped for the best. She did not dare look above or below; either way made her feel like fainting. Not so with Sasmo. He seemed without either nerves or vertigo and went upwards with relentless purpose, never faltering, and here and there using sheer muscular power to raise himself and his burden to the next highest point. It was quite the most amazing feat of gymnastic endurance that Molly had ever known.

And at last the out-jutting disc-like edge of the observatory's parapet was only a few feet overhead. Molly hung on like grim death, wondering how Sasmo was going to circumvent the obstacle. He paused for a moment, surveying — even looking down the two-mile drop below and seeming undisturbed. Then he began to crouch and for a moment Molly had the frightful fear that she was going to slip from his broad back —

Immediately afterwards, however, he flew outwards into the void as though impelled by uncoiling springs. His hands shot outwards and forwards, then he jerked to a comparative standstill and there came the twang of wire. Molly gulped and forced herself to look upwards. She realised now, that Sasmo had chanced everything on a leap into the night and caught hold of the wire down which she had descended. Possibly his sight was keener than an Earthling's. Whatever the answer he now began to haul himself up hand over hand, not even troubling to use his legs to help him.

At last he was creeping over the edge of the parapet, then Molly felt strong hands seizing her and she was lifted from the alien's back and set on her feet. Adam Quirke towered over her, his moonlike face blank in astonishment.

'What's this?' he demanded. 'A sprat to catch a whale?'

Molly doubled her hands against herself and nodded her head towards Sasmo as he straightened up. Except for the fact that he was breathing rather heavily he did not seem much the worse for his efforts.

'Damn me,' Quirke murmured. 'For once I'm taken utterly by surprise! What's happened, light of my life?'

'Pretty well everything.' Molly winced as she spoke. 'I was about falling off the wire when Sasmo saved me . . . ' And she gave the details whilst the alien himself stood calmly looking about him.

'Thanks for what you did for Molly, anyway, Sasmo,' Quirke said briefly. 'Just the same you've plenty of explaining to do. Come down into the observatory: I must have a look at this young lady's hands before anything else.' Sasmo nodded and followed Quirke down the ladder. With Molly over his shoulder since she could not hold the ladder in the normal way, he descended to the observatory floor. In all it took ten minutes, with the observatory's first-aid kit, to bind up Molly's hands, then, as she settled in one of the normal chairs Quirke turned and looked at the alien. He looked back, unflinching, with his cold green eyes, his scratch of a mouth compressed to the limit.

'How do you explain your behaviour?' Quirke demanded. 'I appreciate your saving the life of my secretary and bringing her back here to safety, but that cannot be weighed against the fact that you had no right to be anywhere near the column or the observatory.'

'I think otherwise,' Sasmo answered

deliberately. 'Because the Commissioner of Police came to my apartment this evening and as good as accused me of the murder of Dr. Brunner. Whilst he did not actually arrest me I gathered enough to realise that he might do so before long. It therefore seemed expedient to me that I should come to the observatory secretly and examine it with a view to finding the real killer.'

'And you preferred to use the external means of entry rather than let the janitor see you?'

'Exactly.'

'How did you get past the watchman in the entrance hall?'

Sasmo gave his thin, hard smile. 'At no point did I enter the column, Mr. Quirke. I climbed up the outside, including the first half. I was resolved that nobody should see me.'

'As it happened the observatory roof was open. How would you have fared had it not been?'

'There are windows. I could easily have forced one of them. I know exactly what kind of catches they have.'

'And the constable who is on duty?' Quirke enquired. 'Did you propose to make yourself invisible?'

For answer Sasmo felt in his jacket pocket and produced what looked like an ordinary aspirin tablet. He held his broad palm forward, the tablet in the centre of it. 'I would have entered without being seen; I would have taken good care of that. After I had located the constable's position I would have tossed this tablet towards him. It breaks instantly upon hitting anything and releases an invisible, far-reaching vapour, which, as far as Earth people are concerned, brings unconsciousness of from one to three hours. Meantime the pellet dilquesces. The constable would have recovered to find nothing to explain his unconsciousness. His only conclusion could be that he had unexpectedly fainted . . . '

Sasmo put the pellet back in his pocket. 'Oh, yes, Mr. Quirke, I had everything worked out.'

'Except the fact that I happen to be here. Had you known of that you would surely not have acted.'

'True,' Sasmo admitted, unabashed. 'From the ground the rim of the parapet prevents one seeing — when near to — whether or not the observatory is lighted. It seems to me fortunate that I came along as I did, otherwise you would now have been without a secretary.'

'I have already expressed my appreciation of your help in that respect, but unfortunately you make things difficult for me, Sasmo . . . Let us assume that you had made your climb without having encountered Molly on the way. What would you have done at discovering I was within this observatory? Thrown a pellet at me?'

'Not at all. I would have behaved as I am doing now. You are a man of high intelligence and able to appreciate my motives. I cannot say the same of the constable.'

Quirke did not comment for a moment. He was doing his utmost to weigh up this inscrutable being of Procyon — and failing magnificently. Of all the alien creatures walking Earth in this day and age, Sasmo took the palm for being enigmatically individual.

'You have spoken of finding the real killer,' Quirke said at last, moving to the nearest chair and settling his ponderous weight upon it. 'Have you any reason to suspect anybody in particular?'

'Not in the least. I merely felt that if I looked about me and exerted my intelligence I might find something definite which would deflect the Commissioner's suspicions from me.'

'I see. Did the Commissioner give any specific reason why he should suspect you more than the others involved?'

'No. As I understood him, all of us are equally involved. I assume that Miss Adley and Mr. Calhoun are prepared to accept accusation and do nothing about it. I am not. I am a man of high integrity even if I am an alien, and I refuse to tolerate anything which is either a slur upon my character or my technical ability.'

'As I understand it,' Quirke said, closing his eyes under the effort of recollection; 'you have an airtight alibi for last night. When you left here you went to the Interplanetary Club on Hundredth Street and stayed there until half past three this morning. You spent the time in the club library making notes from the books. I have the Commissioner's word on that, so how can he possibly attach suspicion to you?'

'When I gave my story to the Commissioner — or it least to his enquiring busybodies — I did not state the time at which I left the Club. That was obtained later by the police themselves and the night-commissionaire informed them that I was there until half-past three. I was not. I left at two o'clock and went home. The mistake arose through the commissionaire's watch having got out of order and gained considerably. It was only when the commissionaire realised that I must have been at home *before* half past three, in order to have received the janitor's phone call, that he looked into it. When he found the error he jumped to the conclusion I could have done almost anything from two o'clock onwards.'

'And *did* you do anything?' Quirke demanded.

'No. I give you my word on that.'

Quirke sighed and got to his feet. 'You make it hard for me, Sasmo . . . You have demonstrated, albeit accidentally, that you are capable of climbing a column two miles high and that you have superhuman strength. Those two factors alone are enough to fit the case. There is even the motive . . . You did not like Dr. Brunner because he questioned your ability in regard to technical efficiency. Yet in spite of these things I want to believe in you.'

'Thank you,' Sasmo responded politely. 'Will you give me permission to examine this observatory and see if I can spot anything which you may have missed?'

Quirke spread his hands. 'By all means, if you do find anything unusual call me at my home — Main seven two. I have enough faith in you to let you roam as you please. I would, however, like your assurance that you will not try to overpower the constable over there.'

'I promise you that, Mr. Quirke.'

Quirke seemed satisfied. He turned and

lumbered over to where Molly was sitting white-faced and screwed up, her arms tightly folded.

'Time we went home, m'dear,' Quirke said seriously. 'And I think a call at the hospital might be a good notion.'

Molly shook her head resolutely. 'No need for that, A.Q. I'll be all right. When I get home Mrs. Alroyd will see I'm looked after.'

'I can't be sorry enough,' Quirke muttered. 'Would it be any good if I bent down and let you take a free kick? You couldn't possibly miss!'

Quirke hovered on the verge of one of his paroxysms but for once held it in check as he saw Molly's taut expression. Reaching down his hand he helped her to her feet and threw her coat about her shoulders. With a final glance back at the prowling Sasmo and puzzled policeman they left the observatory, taking their farewell of the janitor as they went to the elevator.

They were in the car, Quirke driving, before Molly made any comment.

'Sorry I bungled things, A.Q. I didn't

think I'd do it that badly. First time I've let you down.'

'Don't be too sure that you did, light of my life. But for your spectacular feat we wouldn't have known anything about Sasmo's capabilities. The damn' man's a revelation.'

'If you suspect he may have done the job why did you let him roam the observatory?'

'I didn't say anything about suspecting him. In fact I think he's entirely innocent because I still maintain that, had he intended to kill Brunner, he would have been much more scientific in his approach. I've let him wander around the observatory because he may find something we've missed. Remember he is not an Earthman with Earthly senses. He may find it possible to detect something that completely eludes us. In other words, let him do the work for us.'

'I see. Well, here's to hoping.'

After which Molly said no more, chiefly because she was in too much pain to think clearly. Quirke saw to it that she was safely delivered at her apartment, and into the care of Mrs. Alroyd, the proprietress of the entire block of self-service apartments.

'And if you're no better tomorrow,' Quirke said, as he took his leave of the girl, 'I'll send a specialist to put you right. Don't worry about your work: I'll keep going.'

'I'll be there as usual!' Molly said firmly. 'You don't suppose I want to miss the fun, do you?'

Quirke smiled and went on his way. Returning home, he spent a couple of hours with his wife and behaved exactly like any normal man, never once referring to the matters absorbing his attention. He never discussed his cases with his wife, mainly because she was utterly unscientific and because, in her heart of hearts, she had the dim suspicion that her husband was slightly crazy. Evelyn Quirke had never heard of that fine division which lies between madness and genius otherwise she might have fathomed her husband more easily.

It was after midnight when Quirke set in work again, no idea of retiring to bed ever entering his head. He went into his laboratory, donned his alpaca jacket, then lighted his favourite briar. An all-night session was foreshadowed . . . correctly. He sat in the comfortable warmth hour after hour, only the solitary low-power lamp burning, his mind weaving in and out of the problem, discarding this and accepting that. It was in the early hours when he finally stirred and went across to the books he had brought in during the day from the library. *The Mutated Fauna of Mars* was the one that finally came in for his attention, giving as it did all the details of the Martian gossamer-spider, which information he had already more or less absorbed.

'Spin because they have to,' he muttered, gazing absently into the shadows. 'In the process of which an intangible odour is given forth reminiscent of over-ripe pineapple. Actually the odour of excretia from the insect, but by no means offensive and, indeed, used by certain interplanetary firms as the basis of hair perfume . . . '

Quirke laid aside the book and

reflected. 'Attracted by a bright and polished surface, but not by light itself. Now I *wonder* . . . '

He frowned, conjuring up a mental vision of Brunner's body as he had seen it in the photographic record — that fearful gash across the forehead, the bruise marks on the throat. And then the bloodstain on the manual arm of the telescope. And the scratches on the mirror?

Suddenly he made up his mind and reached to the telephone. That it was in the small hours did not concern him as he dialled the private number of the Commissioner of Police and then waited for the answer.

It came at last — sleepy and mumbling. 'Yes? Police Commissioner speaking.'

'Sorry to disturb your beauty sleep, Commissioner. Quirke here, full of a good idea.'

'Oh, *you*! Dammit, man, can't it wait until morning?'

'It *is* morning, even though the sun isn't up. Now listen: I have arrived at the conclusion that your police surgeon was never more wrong in his life than when he declared Dr. Brunner died from either a blow on the head or manual strangulation.'

There were noises like incipient apoplexy at the other end.

'Carter's never been wrong in his career, Quirke, and there is no reason why he should start being so now! Go to bed and sleep it off!'

'Carter,' Quirke said deliberately, 'merely inferred death from those two causes because his medical knowledge could not carry him any further. I've delved much deeper and I stick to my opinion that Brunner died from some other cause.'

'And the blow on the head and throat marks were put there for fun, I suppose?'

'I'll explain those convincingly enough when I have the rest of the picture in focus. Right now I want your permission to have Brunner exhumed and brought to my laboratory. I intend to conduct a second post mortem with special instruments.'

Long silence, then, 'My God, Quirke, the things you ask for! But I suppose I'll have to satisfy you. How soon do you want the body?'

'By noon at the latest. You can get a special permit rushed through the Home Secretary's office. I'm not exactly unknown when it comes to requiring legal sanction.'

'Very well, I'll do that — but I haven't the remotest idea what you're getting at. Do you mean that one of the four suspects used something unorthodox in order to bring about Brunner's death?'

'Mebbe,' Quirke replied vaguely. 'I can tell you a lot more when I've made my examination of the corpse. Candidly, Commissioner, I think we've been barking up the wrong tree all this time. We've accepted the obvious — or at least you have. When I found myself getting into the same rut I spent a few hours doing nothing but thinking, and damned hard! Out of it came this new conception.'

'Mm. Well, I hope it's justified or the Home Secretary will be more than sarcastic. Incidentally, I've got a new lead of my own.' The Commissioner sounded thoroughly awake now. 'I find that Sasmo, that alien menace, wasn't at his club when — '

'I know. He told me.'

'Huh? Told you? When?'

'I met him tonight at the observatory. For your information he had climbed up the two-mile column from the outside and never turned a hair!'

'That settles it! It must be him and not Calhoun! I'm calling headquarters immediately and having a warrant — '

'Wait!' Quirke interrupted patiently. 'Think this one out first, as I did. It took him exactly one hour to climb a distance of one mile, though I admit he was somewhat laden. Reckon half an hour under normal circumstances and a whole hour to climb the full two miles. Right! Now, around three o'clock — mark that! — the janitor heard what we assume was Brunner's death cry. He almost immediately rang up Sasmo, Monica Adley, and Calhoun, certainly not later than three-thirty. Sasmo answered the call and came to the observatory. How did he do that if it

152

would take him at least an hour to descend the column's exterior?'

'All right, you win,' the Commissioner growled. 'Are you dead sure of the timing, though?'

'Perfectly. I had my watch in my hand and calculated — not for Sasmo, but for Molly Brayson; she was swinging on a wire outside the column.'

'She was *what*? What in blazes was she doing that for?'

'Never mind — just more of my experimenting and if it proved nothing else it showed that Sasmo couldn't have been guilty. We can't get away from the fact, Commissioner, that none of those concerned could have committed the murder and got away without being seen by the janitor, and he is ruled out, it seems, by his age and general feebleness compared to the strength of Brunner.'

'Then who *did* do it? Must have been somebody!'

'Or something,' Quirke said ambiguously. 'Anyway, get that permit through, Commissioner, and I'll be your friend for life!'

And with that, he rang off and calmly went to bed . . .

★ ★ ★

Towards ten o'clock the following morning Quirke learned over the 'phone that his application for the exhumation of Brunner had been granted and that the body would be duly delivered by noon. He had hardly digested this news to his entire satisfaction, before Molly arrived, pale but determined, her hands projecting from the wide sleeves of her coat like small white footballs, so thick was the bandaging.

'Honestly, light of my life, you can take time off if you want,' Quirke told her seriously. 'Even sue me if you like for not taking proper care of you.'

'Sue nothing, A.Q. I'm no child and I slid down that wire with my eyes wide open. I'll be all right though don't expect me to write anything. The doc says I'll be a week with these bandages: by then gloves will do. Filthy mess I made of my palms, I'm afraid.'

'Too bad,' Quirke said sympathetically. 'However, if it's any consolation to you, you were instrumental in proving that Sasmo was not the one who killed Brunner.'

'Oh? How do you make that out?'

Quirke repeated what he had told the Commissioner as he helped Molly off with her coat. When he had finished she gave him a puzzled look.

'Then what do you suggest we do, then? Start looking into Monica Adley's movements? She's the only one left in the running now. You've disposed of the janitor, Sasmo, and Calhoun — at least to your own satisfaction — but you haven't paid much attention to Monica.'

'Nor shall I. Not unless my present theory goes completely down the drain. I cannot for a moment picture a girl like Monica Adley battering Brunner. Doesn't make sense ... No, I remain sure now that a different reason to any yet thought of caused Brunner's death — and the terror he experienced. We shall see when the second postmortem is complete — ' Quirke broke off as the televisor equipment linked the photo-electric cell on the front drive came into action. Immediately there came the sound of footsteps in the speaker and then on the screen a vision of a square figure, thick-necked, with a perfectly round head.

'Sasmo!' Molly exclaimed in surprise. 'What on earth can he want?'

Quirke switched on the microphone. 'Enter, Mr. Sasmo, if you please. Straight down the hall to the door marked 'Private'.'

It was typical of the stolid, inscrutable alien that he took the radio-directed order with complete calmness. When the front door had opened he obeyed instructions and in another moment or two appeared in the laboratory. He gave a deferential bow of the head towards Molly.

'I trust your hands are a little less painful today, Miss Brayson?'

'Just numb and smarty,' Molly smiled. 'And now I'm feeling more normal I'd like to thank you most sincerely for everything you did for me last night. You saved my life, you know, and that is something.'

'I trust,' the man from Procyon responded, 'that it will cause Mr. Quirke to think more kindly of me. To save a life is so much more important than to destroy one.'

'Meaning,' Quirke said, 'that the fact you saved my secretary's life makes it obvious that you have no homicidal tendencies?'

'At the very least,' Sasmo murmured, 'it is a logical inference.'

Quirke pondered for a moment, then smiled disarmingly. 'And the reason for your visit, Mr. Sasmo?'

'Partly to enquire after Miss Brayson's health and partly to report on my observatory investigation. Much to my disappointment I failed to discover anything valuable in the way of evidence. I thought you would like to know that.'

'Yes, I am glad to know it,' Quirke admitted. 'Not that it comes as a surprise, however. I went over that observatory pretty thoroughly myself, and so did the police. However, if you are worried over the police accusation concerning yourself you need not be. I have positive proof of your innocence and have told the Commissioner as much.'

'Positive proof?' The alien looked vaguely surprised. 'For a man of your intelligence, Mr. Quirke, that's a very dogmatic assertion.'

'Not without reason, Mr. Sasmo. I have weighed all the evidence and, all things being equal, I do not believe you had a thing to do with Dr. Brunner's murder.'

'And what of the others equally open to suspicion?'

'I would prefer not to comment upon them. I have only stated my opinion of how you stand because you are directly concerned.'

'I see — and I am grateful. Since you have been so frank with me I will pass on to you something that may be of use, which I discovered in the observatory. Though I cannot in any way use it myself as evidence you may find something interesting in it. Briefly, there is a distinct perfume in the observatory.'

'There is?' Quirke gave a sharp little

frown. 'I did not notice it. Did you, Molly?'

'Not in the slightest, boss.'

'That,' Sasmo said, 'is perhaps because the olfactory organs of Earth human beings are not very strongly developed, as is the case with your animal kingdom. However, since your Earth women have the peculiar tendency to wear perfume, it occurred to me that the presence of perfume might suggest a . . . woman.'

'Only one woman connected with the observatory,' Molly put in, 'and that's Monica Adley.'

'Exactly.' Sasmo looked at her with his relentless green eyes.

'Do you use perfume, m'dear?' Quirke asked vaguely. 'If you do I never noticed it.'

'A trace — not much.'

'The perfume I can detect at the moment is not the same as the one in the observatory,' Sasmo said. 'I assume, Mr. Quirke, that your query is concerned with the fact that you and Miss Brayson have been in the observatory and that she might have left the perfumed aroma behind?'

'That was my guess,' Quirke admitted. 'But now you have dispelled it. Let us take the matter a stage further. You have worked beside Miss Adley for a long time, so you must have been aware if she used perfume — '

'Up to now,' Sasmo interrupted, 'she has always used Marloti Essence — a most exquisite perfume. It lingers in the observatory even yet. But overriding it is a stronger perfume, elusive yet nonetheless distinct. I would liken it to your Earthly pineapple. A most peculiar scent for a fastidious woman to use.'

'Most peculiar,' Quirke admitted, distance in his eyes. 'Can you tell me something, Mr. Sasmo — was this pineapple odour more distinct in one place than another?'

'It seemed to me that it was. Whilst it pervaded most of the observatory it was particularly noticeable in the corners and very strong indeed at one part of the dome parapet.'

'Really?' Quirke's eyes had suddenly brightened. 'In the vicinity of the reflector, perhaps?'

'Now you mention it, yes.'

Silence. Quirke was smiling amiably to himself, looking oddly like a fat schoolboy who has found a well-stocked larder.

'Do you attach some special significance to the fact that the aroma was more distinct in the dome parapet?' Sasmo asked. 'Or are you basing your inference on the fact that most odours have a tendency to rise upwards with warm air?'

'Just a theory,' Quirke responded vaguely. 'Nothing more . . . And I am indebted to you, Mr. Sasmo — very indebted. Is there anything else you wish to tell me?'

"I think not, but I shall leave here with the pleasurable knowledge that you at least believe in my innocence.'

Upon which Sasmo gave his taut little bow to Molly and then took his departure. Quirke saw him out, then returned to the laboratory with absorption on his moonlike face. Molly did not ask any questions: she just waited. And sure enough Quirke presently came round to voicing his meditations.

'For your information, light of my life a gossamer-spider excretes an odour reminiscent of over-ripe pineapple. Need I say more?'

Molly shrugged. 'What of it? That spider was always in the observatory, hence Brunner's anger with old Joe. That the insect left its aroma behind in the corners is nothing unusual. Far as I can gather it always spun its web in the corners where there was a double brightness of wall to attract it.'

'Quite so, but in this case the brightness of the reflector and particularly the object glass no doubt, had attracted it! Otherwise the aroma could not have been so strong up on the dome parapet. I don't think the aroma was on the parapet *itself* but around or near the reflector's object glass. If you recall we left the object glass level with the parapet when I had finished examining it — and found nothing . . . We move nearer, m'dear, much nearer!'

'I wish I could see in what way!'

'You will in time. First let me examine the cadaver that was Brunner. From that I may be able to determine if this new theory I have in mind is correct — '

Quirke glanced up as the p.e.c. warning system on the house drive gave its signal. He looked into the sound-screen and beheld four men approaching bearing on their shoulders a completely plain coffin. Behind them came the Metropolitan Commissioner himself, dogged and bothered-looking. Beyond him again in the distance stood the police black maria in which the body had evidently been conveyed.

'Maybe the Commissioner doesn't trust me,' Quirke grinned. 'Wants to see for himself what I'm up to. All right, he shall!' He switched on the microphone and snapped the front door switch. Come right in, Commissioner — you know your way by now!'

After a moment or two the Commissioner entered. The four men put down the coffin on the nearby long table, as directed by Quirke, then the gigantic scientist turned and eyed the Commissioner in some amusement.

'What's the matter, Commissioner?

Don't you trust me with a corpse?'

'You know me better than that, Quirke — 'Morning, Miss Brayson. I'm simply here because the law is that a police officer must be present when an exhumed body is examined by somebody outside of the police service. These men here are not policemen, either — so I represent the legal side.'

'And doubtless hope for first hand information at the same time?'

'I'll not deny it,' the Commissioner answered. 'I've got to be knowing how long you're intending to fool around. My superiors are already wanting to know what the devil I'm doing all this time; and as for the Press — !'

Quirke did not say anything. He motioned the four coffin bearers to chairs and then unscrewed the coffin lid. For a moment or two he stood looking down on the dead face of Brunner.

'What part of the body do you want to examine?' the Commissioner asked, coming forward.

'Just his head. The Penetrator should tell me all I want to know.'

'What's a Penetrator? One of your fancy instruments?'

'It's an instrument, yes — but it isn't fancy.' Quirke shook for a second or two with inward amusement and then crossed to an object that seemed to be a hybrid of a lightstand, a cine-camera, an arc-lamp, and a ground-glass screen. Certainly it wasn't 'fancy.' On the contrary it looked quite terrifying.

'The basic principle of this is X-ray,' Quirke explained, dragging the equipment forward. 'It is considerably advanced on that, however, since it can be adjusted to photograph accurately any internal part of a body. We do not get a shadow silhouette as in the normal X-ray photograph, but a complete and understandable picture. If I wished,' Quirke finished, his eyes starting to dance again, 'I could accept millions from the Metropolitan Hospital for this invention. On the strength of that I could retire and grow black daffodils.'

'Why black ones?' The Commissioner was staring blankly.

'Because all daffodils would go into

mourning once I began to experiment on them.'

The laboratory trembled. Molly yawned slightly behind one of her bandaged hands and the Commissioner scratched the back of his neck. The four coffin bearers looked at one another — then at last, tears swimming in his eyes, Quirke had manoeuvred to angle his Penetrator into the position he desired — which was directly in line with Brunner's head.

'The energy emanated from this instrument will pass through the wood of the coffin and Brunner's skullbone,' Quirke explained, intensely serious once more. 'After that, just watch for yourselves.'

The Commissioner and Molly both nodded, and the four coffin bearers were also interested enough to rise and come forward. Quirke adjusted the controls on the complicated panel and then switched on the power. Almost immediately the scanner-screen of the Penetrator glowed into life and, as Quirke manipulated the knobs and rheostats, the effect was as if a camera were travelling straight through the coffin woodwork and into Brunner's skull. The extraordinary thing about the whole demonstration was that the images were picked up and were brightly lighted. How he achieved this effect Quirke did not explain, beyond a vague deference to thermostatic control of light photons — which could have meant just anything.

'Mm, he had quite a well-developed brain,' Quirke commented, as the interior of the dead astronomer's head was laid bare. 'Excellent convolutions and sound neuronic system — but do you notice that, Commissioner?'

The Commissioner found himself looking at a V-shaped sheath of fibre set dead between the two hemispheres of the brain. The sheath had a curiously burned and shrivelled appearance.

'Doesn't look too healthy,' he commented. 'What part of the brain is it, anyway?'

'The optic nerve, and there's no doubt of the fact that it has been burned out. You will also notice that where it connects to the brain itself there is a severe blistering and scoring as though a red-hot wire had been gouging.'

'You're right . . . ' The Commissioner leaned forward and examined the screen intently. 'Definitely right! But it still does not make sense!'

'Not to you, perhaps: it does to me.' Quirke lingered again over the magical reproduction of the interior of Brunner's head, then at length he switched off and reflected.

'Well? Well?' the Commissioner demanded impatiently. 'How far does this get us? What have we seen here that is strong enough evidence to prevent me arresting Calhoun?'

'Calhoun? I thought you'd decided on Sasmo.'

'I had until you showed me it was impossible. That only leaves Calhoun for it. Don't you understand, Quirke? I've got to have some action — and quickly!'

'You'll get it — probably by tomorrow. I've seen enough now to bolster up my new theory, and a most extraordinary one it is. But then, Adam Quirke is never interested in *ordinary* matters.'

'When you've finished blowing your trumpet, how about telling me what the theory is?'

'The theory is that Dr. Brunner was not murdered by anybody at all, but by something and that something, near as dammit, is probably a Martian gossamer-spider owned by one Joe, janitor.'

'What! How the blazes could a spider kill Brunner? It isn't even in the realm of possibility! I've seen gossamer-spiders many a time, read up about 'em too, and they're as frail as a puffball and completely non-poisonous. Have a heart, A.Q.!'

'I have, and a fatty one.' Quirke grinned widely. 'The fact that a gossamer-spider is frail and innocuous has nothing to do with it: there's also another factor connected with the insect which I believe will answer everything. I'm not telling you about that, though, until I've satisfied myself that I'm right — which should be by tomorrow. No use having you Metro boys laughing your heads off if I've guessed wrongly.'

'Wrong isn't the word for it! I suppose the spider bashed in Brunner's head and put the bruise marks on his throat?'

'Hardly.'

The Commissioner hesitated on the edge of another outburst; then he controlled himself. Quirke was obviously not going to say anything to help him.

'Perhaps,' the Commissioner said, thinking, 'I might be able to get some light in the darkness if I can determine why Brunner's optic nerves should be burned out.'

'That is almost the answer,' Quirke replied. 'Not only the optic nerves were destroyed but part of the brain as well. *That* was the cause of death — excruciating pain and overwhelming shock. The blow on the head and the grip on the throat had nothing to do with it. Which reminds me, I've a further test to make of Brunner, something which your boys could not deal with, with their limited instruments.'

The Commissioner did not respond to this sally: he was too busy trying to sort the problem out. Absently he watched Quirke as he moved away his X-ray photographic apparatus and instead wheeled into position what appeared to be a modified version of the electron-microscope.

6

Quirke Takes a Risk

'The gossamer-spider,' Quirke said, as he fiddled with the controls of this new instrument, 'is a remarkable insect in many ways. You say you've read up about it. What do you think of the bit about its web appearing solid to the eye, yet actually being transparent to light?'

'What do I think about it? Nothing much: why should I?'

'You don't even find it fascinating that the web can split what seems — to the eye — to be ordinary white light into its normal spectrum colours?'

'Nothing fascinating in it to me. Beautiful phenomenon, maybe, but hardly relevant.'

Quirke sighed. 'It's a big shame that you Metro boys don't know more about scientific things: you'd get on much better. However, let's try something a little more down-to-earth for the moment . . . '

He elevated his instrument so that the downward pointing lens was directly trained on the corpse's neck. Loosening the collarette from about the throat so that the grey-white flesh was exposed, still with the bruise-marks upon it since the blood had become stagnant and, if anything, had made the marks all the more obvious, Quirke peered through the eyepieces of his strange instrument.

'Make a note, Commissioner,' he said, without glancing up. 'I'd have Molly do it only her hands are out of action — Ready? Two whorl, four arch, ten loop — sixteen down and — er — twenty two across.'

The Commissioner jotted down the items, his brow wrinkled, then with a broad grin Quirke withdrew from the instrument and motioned to it.

'Like to see how those marks look under these lenses?'

The Commissioner did not hesitate. When he came to look through the eyepieces he gave a gasp of surprise.

There before him were the bruise marks — but they were not indeterminate smudges, which even the strongest microscope failed to delineate. They were clearly marked out in whirligig lines, coils, and straight lines, with flat grey patches in between.

'Off hand,' the Commissioner said, looking up, 'I'd say these are distinct fingerprints.'

'They are,' Quirke agreed calmly.

'But how do you get them so uncannily clear? We tried every device we've got and couldn't get anything but smudges.'

'Because, my dear man, you used straight lenses. These lenses are operating through infra-red slides which iron out a great deal of the unwanted portions and leave the rest vividly clear. Just a principle of long-distance photography brought up to date. It is the filtration which makes the difference.'

'It's a damned clever notion!'

'Not particularly. Art experts have been using infra-red filters in their lenses for long enough to detect a spurious painting from an original. This is merely an adaptation with what one might call the 'Quirke touch'.'

'And does it prove anything?' The Commissioner moved from the instrument and watched Quirke as, taking first the left and then the right hand of the corpse he obtained prints therefrom. Because the flesh was dead and therefore not pliable, the prints were not particularly clear — but Quirke seemed satisfied enough.

'Take a seat, Commissioner,' he invited. 'This may take a moment or two.'

The Commissioner perched himself on the edge of the nearby bench and contented himself with watching Quirke's enormous form as he seated himself at a corner desk and began to pore carefully over the prints he had made. Ever and again he measured them against a graph line and then referred to the notations that the Commissioner had written down. In all, this took him twenty minutes; then he went to work with a camera.

First he photographed the marks on the neck through the infra-red lenses; then he photographed the prints he had actually made of the hands. The remainder was automatic process photography by which he finally had in his hands a dual slide on each side of which were the two sets of prints, one from the neck and the other from the fingerprint card. He studied them and then smiled.

'This is going to surprise you a great deal, Commissioner,' he remarked dryly. 'Just as it would have surprised me had I not realised in time that I was heading along the wrong trail. Just take a look at this . . . '

Turning, he closed the window shutters and then switched on a slide projector. Upon a screen hanging on the far wall there appeared the two sets of prints with a black line down the middle. By a simple process of adjustment Quirke finally brought the two sets of prints so that they were parallel — and the remarkable thing was that every line joined exactly!

'From the look of that,' the Commissioner said, astonished, 'the two sets of prints appear to belong to the same person!'

'They do.' Quirke's voice was serenely

calm in the reflected light. 'On the left slide you see the prints photographed from the neck: on the right slide you see the print I made from Brunner's right hand. The two left prints conjoin as well, but that does not signify. If these match, the others cannot fail to — and I hardly need labour the point that no two people in the world have identical finger-prints . . . '

'But these are *Brunner's* fingerprints!'

'Correct.'

'But how can they be? He wouldn't strangle himself! I never heard of a case where anybody committed suicide by manual strangulation. In fact it's physi-cally impossible. As the strength fails the grip weakens and recovery comes — Quirke, what the devil are you driving at?'

Quirke sighed. 'What a gift you have, man, for missing the point! I don't know why I waste valuable time trying to show you the finer points of scientific analysis. I have told you time and time again that Brunner did not die because of strangula-tion, therefore the marks on his neck do not represent any attempt in that direction. What they do represent is the mad, desperate clutching of a man at his throat as he realises he is dying. It is the final convulsive grip of a man trying to get air as his pulses seize up. It is the grip of a man in the torment of indescribable pain. It is the grip of a man on the brink of death.'

There was silence. Quirke switched off his instrument and the touch of a button restored daylight to the laboratory. For once his big, triple-chinned face was not smiling. He was coldly sombre, his china-blue eyes looking steadily at the Commissioner.

'You are sure of these facts, Quirke? I'm completely in your hands now, remember, for you've travelled so far with this new theory of yours I've just got to believe it. But if you go wrong you'll have to explain it to my superiors. I'll never be able to.'

'The fingerprint analysis is conclusive,' Quirke answered. 'Brunner alone caused those bruise marks. Just as conclusive are the evidences of his damaged brain and destroyed optic nerves. We're on the look-out for something of incredible danger, Commissioner, a something which has never been suspected as ever being dangerous.'

'The gossamer-spider?'

'I believe so.'

'I still can't see the connection, but I certainly cannot disprove what you've shown me so far. For all that there is the blow on the head to be explained, and until it is I'm entitled to cling to my suspects. Brunner could have been hit violently over the head and then clutched his throat in anguish.'

Quirke moved irritably. 'Oh, dammit man, where's your imagination? Death came through brain damage, not through the blow. Death was not instantaneous, either. Brunner lived long enough to experience a few moments of sheer exquisite anguish — if I can use such a phrase . . . The blow on the head? Well, I'm almost sure how that happened but I'll tell you better tomorrow. For the time being just digest what I've told you and I'll give you the remainder after experimenting further.'

'You can't do anything before tomorrow, I suppose? Time's flying and I'm expected to make an arrest — '

'If you make an arrest you'll finish up the biggest fool in London. On the other hand if you hold your fire you can use my final analysis how you wish and make a hero out of yourself. I don't want plaudits — only my expenses.'

Quirke grinned, then he rumbled and chuckled. All of a sudden the grim scientist with the analytical brain had vanished and he was the cheerful, obese schoolboy again.

'What sort of an experiment do you propose to make?' The Commissioner rose from the edge of the bench.

'I'm going to try and re-enact what *might* have happened to Brunner on the fateful night.'

'Can I come too? I have *some* connection with the business.'

Quirke hesitated, then shrugged his vast shoulders. 'All right, I can't stop you anyhow. Be at the observatory tonight at eight o'clock, and meantime pray for fine weather.'

★ ★ ★

Whether the Commissioner prayed for fine weather or not he did not say, but the fact remained that when he met Quirke and Molly at the Column entrance at eight that evening the night was clear and cold with the April stars sharply brilliant overhead.

'I'm here just for the ride,' Molly explained, as they went past the night watchman to the elevator. 'I can't write down anything, so I'm next to useless.'

'Not to me, m'dear,' Quirke told her. 'Occasionally you see things which I don't, and besides I may need you for a witness.'

'A witness of what?'

'My death. It may become your sacred duty to inform the world that I died voluntarily trying to solve a mystery.'

As the elevator began to rise, Molly waited for the cyclone of merriment which should normally have followed this statement, but to her surprise it did not come, she looked at Quirke in the dim overhead light and saw his face was

180

grimly serious under the sprouting mane of white hair.

'You really *mean* it, boss?' she asked in alarm.

'Of course I do! In repeating Brunner's exact movements with what I believe caused his death I am compelled to face the same danger. I cannot ask for a volunteer — nor would I — but I am nevertheless determined to carry this problem through to the finish. So by this time tomorrow the world may be minus Adam Quirke. I shan't mind, but the world will,' Quirke finished, with a touch of his normal ponderous humour.

'I don't like this business at all,' the Commissioner complained. 'No guarantee you're right, either. Why risk your life when there's a normal suspect to pick on?'

'And let an innocent person pay the penalty? Shame on you, Commissioner! Your job's making you heartless.'

The Commissioner shrugged and the subject was dropped as the elevator reached the top of the column. The three crossed the narrow corridor and entered

Joe's quarters to find him munching an early supper. He scrambled to his feet as the trio entered.

'Well, I'm glad of some different company at last!' he exclaimed. 'What with me stuck here and that one copper on guard in the observatory, and neither of us knowin' who killed Dr. Brunner, it gets a bit 'ard on the nerves.'

'Where's Loony?' Quirke asked briefly, looking about him — and the janitor looked surprised.

'I ain't quite sure, Mr. Quirke, but 'e must be about somewhere. Always makin' off somewhere. That was what got Dr. Brunner so sore.'

'I'm aware of that. Wherever Loony is, find him. I think I can make use of that insect.'

'You can?' The janitor looked puzzled. 'Darned if I can see how!'

'What you can see, Joe, is not of the least interest to us,' the Commissioner snapped. 'Find that damned spider and hurry up about it!'

The janitor shrugged then shambled off into the various corners of his modest living quarters.

Finally, from the little bedroom, he brought Loony into view. The beautiful insect was suspended from his gnarled hand by means of a ropy, hair-edged thread and its enormous glistening eyes were watching Quirke, Molly, and the Commissioner intently. Molly gave a little shiver as the alien appearance of this immigrant from Mars scared her for a moment.

'There 'e is!' Joe exclaimed proudly. 'Good old Loony! The only pal I've got.'

'May I take him?' Quirke asked, extending his hand.

'Aye — if 'e'll take to you. Can but try, I s'pose.'

Evidently the insect was not having any, however. It refused all Quirke's invitations and remained dangling from the thread cast about its master's hand.

'Very well then,' Quirke decided. 'Bring him up into the observatory, Joe. I want to try something.'

Joe nodded and began to climb the ladder to the observatory above. He had just reached the top, the others following behind, when Loony suddenly decided to cast his anchorage. He darted away across the floor, his many hairy legs moving swiftly. As on other occasions he finished up in a corner and began his usual activity of swiftly weaving a dense web of incomparable beauty.

'I'll soon stop 'im,' Joe volunteered, but Quirke caught at his shoulder.

'No, wait a moment. I want to watch what he does.'

'Up to you, Mr. Quirke. That's the one thing I can't understand about Loony — 'e's always making webs. 'Tisn't as though there's any insects for him to catch. Just seems to be a sort of 'obby with 'im. I wouldn't mind so much if I didn't 'ave to spend half my life cleanin' the webs up after 'im.'

'Weaving webs is not a hobby, Joe,' Quirke said. 'It's a necessity. If he didn't weave them he'd die. It's a natural excretion which has to be performed.'

'All this may be very interesting,' the Commissioner put in impatiently, 'but when all's said and done we're not ento- mologists! Can't we get started, Quirke?'

'In a moment, Commissioner ... '
Quirke watched the insect as it wove its intricate web with incredible speed, then he sniffed gently at the air.

'Pineapple,' Molly said. 'I notice it too, but only by making an effort to do so. No doubt it's there.'

'Pineapple?' Joe repeated. 'Oh, sure — that's Loony, 'e always makes a smell like pineapple when 'e weaves a web. Must be the stuff itself, I s'pose.'

Quirke apparently decided at last to get on the move. He went over to the corner where the spider was operating, then selecting an appropriate moment caught at the main thread and swept it up in his fingers. As a result, the entire web — as far as it had been created — together with the spider was lifted in his hand. Holding his arm aloft Quirke peered through the web intently, studying the observatory lamps through it. All he beheld was a spectrum of the lamps instead of a flood of white light.

The Commissioner and Molly came and looked with him, but even when they had finished they were not much wiser.

'You said before that the web splits white light into its correct spectrum colours,' the Commissioner remarked, 'so what is so novel about this? All we are seeing is the spectrum of neon gas through the web from the lamp-tubes up there.'

'Quite so,' Quirke assented, lowering his arm, 'and it satisfies me that light of what we call the normal type is by no means dangerous when filtered through this web. So the answer must lie in Betelgeuse itself.'

The Commissioner opened his mouth and then shut it again. He just did not know any more where he was. The only alternative was to wait for Quirke to explain himself. At the moment, though, he did not appear to have any intention of doing so, for he lumbered across to the enormous reflector with the spider dangling from the thread about his hand.

'If you wouldn't mind opening the roof?' he requested, with a glance over his shoulder — and Molly performed this task by knocking the appropriate switches with her elbow. As the hemispheres rolled back Quirke disentangled the spider from the web and then placed it near the reflector. Instantly the polished parts attracted it but it did not seem satisfied to remain at the base of the giant instrument and spin another of its everlasting webs. Instead it sped up the latticed metal length and finally disappeared over the lip of the huge object glass.

'That object glass uncovered?' Quirke asked the janitor quickly, and Joe gave a shrug.

'I wouldn't know, Mr. Quirke. Isn't my job to do that. The reflector's just as you left it last time you were here.'

'Then it will still be uncovered,' Quirke said. 'Far as I can tell it has remained uncovered since Brunner studied Betelgeuse.'

Turning, he moved like a baby elephant towards the ladder that led to the parapet. Puffing and panting he mounted it as rapidly as his tremendous bulk would allow, whilst the Commissioner, Molly, Joe, and the constable on duty watched him in silent bewilderment. For the life of them they could not decide what he was driving at.

Once he gained the narrow parapet ledge, Quirke hurried along to the reflector and then stood gazing at the object glass, which was about level with the ledge. Here indeed the gossamer-spider was having the time if its life, speeding back and forth across the big sunken lens hood, the flawlessly polished surface of the object glass lying beneath it like a miniature lake. Here evidently was one of the brightest surfaces the spider had yet encountered, and judging from the speed at which it was weaving its web its 'emotions' were those of the highest pleasure.

'Anything happening?' the Commissioner demanded from below. 'We seem to be wasting a terrible lot of time, Quirke!'

'Time is relative,' Quirke told him, glancing down. 'I can't make the experiment until Loony has finished his activities.'

'Why not? Dammit, do you mean to tell me that we have to wait for a spider?'

'I do, because at the moment I think he

is doing exactly what he did on the night of Brunner's death: weaving a web across the telescopic object glass, a process quite invisible from below. You, down there, can't see Loony at work, can you?'

Heads shook. Quirke nodded complacently.

'How long will he take, boss?' Molly called up.

'Not long. At the rate he's going at I'd say about ten minutes. In the meantime, Joe, let me ask you something. Where was Loony at the time of Dr. Brunner's death?'

The janitor thought, studying the floor and scratching his stubbly chin. Finally he gave a shrug.

'I can't seem to remember, Mr. Quirke. I was so upset with the things that happened I never even thought about Loony.'

'Yes, I suppose that's understandable,' Quirke admitted. 'I think I can tell you where he was — up here, weaving a web exactly as he is doing now — '

'Wait a minute!' the Commissioner exclaimed. 'I believe I begin to see what you're driving at! The web of that spider is capable of producing the spectra of any type of light: it acts like a sort of filter?'

'That's it,' Quirke agreed. 'And this spider is attracted by highly polished surfaces and is very intelligent. The intelligent part comes in by it weaving a web over the most polished object in the observatory — the telescopic object glass. When the web is complete it will split up the light waves of any object viewed through the reflector. It appears that ordinary light split up by the web has no ill effect, therefore we are led logically to the conclusion that there must be something odd about the light of Betelgeuse when seen in spectrum form.'

'I don't think that's the right answer, A.Q.,' Molly said, thinking.

'Why not, light of my life? I'm always open to suggestions.'

'Well, astronomers have been viewing the spectrum of Betelgeuse for ages and nothing has ever happened to them.'

'That,' Quirke said, 'I have taken into account — but our spectrum readings are made in the normal way through prisms because we have no direct process by which to split up light into its constituent parts. This web is a natural prism and filter combined in that it enables any light-emitting object to be studied straight on, as it were, without the necessity of using a prism. Further, an absolutely true spectrum may contain elements that a man-made contrivance can never capture. Nature is always more exact than we are.'

There was silence. Quirke looked at the dense web that was now spread across the object-glass, then he studied the sky and singled out ruddy Betelgeuse. At length he turned to the ladder and descended once more to the floor of the observatory.

'What happens now I don't quite know,' he said quietly, 'but I propose to set the reflector in action and survey the image of Betelgeuse cast on this mirror here. It will be Betelgeuse as seen through the prismatic filter of that web and it may contain lethal qualities such as killed Dr. Brunner. That is the risk I mentioned, and which I am prepared to take.'

'It's too dangerous a chance to take!' the Commissioner objected. 'Can't you — '

'No,' Quirke told him. 'I can't. I know exactly what I am doing. The rest of you keep away from this mirror. I only intend to take a flashing glimpse and that surely ought not to do any harm.'

Obviously resolved, he turned to the girder that supported the viewing chair and carefully edged his way along it, finally settling in the chair itself. Molly watched him anxiously; the janitor pulled aside the silk velvet mirror cover; and the Commissioner was frowning in the deepest doubt.

'Well,' Quirke said, 'here I go. Stand back, the rest of you.'

He waited until they had done so — then suddenly Molly spoke.

'Just a minute, boss! You haven't worked out the necessary mathematics to make sure the reflector is trained on Betelgeuse! It might be pointing just anywhere!'

'It might be, my love, but it isn't. I worked out the figures whilst I was up on the parapet there waiting for our hairy friend to finish his activities. The reflector is positioned correctly — or at least near enough for our purpose.' Quirke became silent, his stumpy fingers on the chair arms' control buttons. Then suddenly he depressed the switches that allowed the reflector to come into action and cast its image upon the mecuroid mirror.

Quirke shut his eyes and remained motionless for a moment or so. He could feel the perspiration of strain gathering on his forehead and coursing down his face: then he opened his eyes very slightly and looked at the mirror below him. Immediately a swirling scum of colours hit back at him, but he did not experience anything that could be called equivalent to pain or shock.

Satisfied be was still in control, he opened his eyes to the full, though still inwardly prepared for the worst. Nothing happened. His reactions were perfectly normal even if the scene on the mirror was not, for instead of a normal colour reflection of the heavens, with Betelgeuse predominating, it looked as though everything was in a chaotic colour-fog. The stars were distorted into blazing javelins of emerald, green, and yellow, or blue, pink, and amethyst — whilst Betelgeuse himself was a haloed orb of pure ruby red, pouring forth this major colour wavelength to the exclusion of all others. A fascinating, even terrible sight, but certainly not lethal.

'Can we look?' came the tense enquiry of the Commissioner, and Quirke gave a start.

'Yes, of course. Look by all means . . . '

Everybody did so, including the constable in charge. Then they all stood around the edge of the mirror and looked at Quirke enquiringly.

'I just don't understand it!' All the fight seemed to have gone out of Quirke. His gross figure was slumped forward in the chair as he studied the lake of dizzying colours below him. 'The effect I expected is missing. But why? Dammit, *why*?'

7

Volunteer for Death

'I think,' the Commissioner said, 'It's time you stopped playing around with theories, Quirke, and let the law take its course. Mind you, I'm not saying you haven't appeared to be correct up to a point, but where's the use of that if the final result is a failure?'

'Somewhere,' Quirke muttered, half to himself, 'I've missed something, something vital! The effect that killed Brunner was produced through this mirror! I'm convinced of that! So why doesn't it happen now?' He looked up with almost a pleading expression. 'You are sure not one of you feels anything peculiar when looking down on this colour distortion of the stars?'

'Not a thing, boss,' Molly said regretfully, speaking for the others as they shook their heads slowly.

Quirke sighed, struggled out of the chair, then picked his way along the girder back to the observatory floor. Going to the nearest chair he lowered his immense weight into it and sat scowling.

'I'm sorry, Quirke,' the Commissioner said briefly, 'but this is as far as I dare go. I've given you every possible leeway but now I must begin to catch up. In the morning I shall have David Calhoun arrested unless by then you've worked out what is wrong with your theory. A pity really, because I did begin to think you'd got something.'

'There's absolutely nothing wrong with my reasoning because it is the only answer which fits,' Quirke retorted. 'It is the unknown factor which has upset my calculations and I've got to find out what it is . . . ' He looked up suddenly. 'Joe, come here a moment.'

The janitor shuffled across and looked at Quirke enquiringly.

'Tell me . . . ' Quirke hunched forward and breathed hard. 'On what do you feed that fantastic pet of yours?'

'Martian grub food mostly. It's on sale

in most of the pet stores, Mr. Quirke. My Loony isn't the only one of 'is kind y'know.'

'True. There are hundreds of them, I know. Did you feed him on the grub food on the night of Dr. Brunner's murder?'

Joe nodded promptly. 'Certainly I did. Ain't nothin' else I ever uses for 'im.'

'Mm . . . All right, Joe. Thanks.'

The Commissioner watched the janitor mooch away and then looked back at the baffled scientist.

'And what was the point of that enquiry, Quirke? What difference does it make what the beastly insects eat?'

'It might have made all the difference in the world.' Quirke was looking completely baulked. 'I don't have to tell you, do I, that insects — in common with animals and human beings — are governed in physical power according to the nutriment they get? Leave out certain vital ingredients in the diet of an animal, for instance, and he doesn't behave as he normally should. What I was trying to discover was if, on the night of Brunner's death, Loony had had some particular kind of food that had altered the constitution of his web. It could be, you know — but apparently it was not. Loony was in no way unique on the fatal night, which only serves to complicate the problem.'

The Commissioner sighed and buttoned up his overcoat. 'Well, Quirke, I'm sorry, but you seem to have misfired badly on this occasion. I've got to be on my way. I can only hold my hand until morning, then I've just got to act — or maybe lose my job. Good night. 'Night, Miss Brayson.'

Molly mumbled something and Quirke hardly seemed to notice. He was staring up at the reflector from which the gossamer-spider was now emerging, its webwork over the telescopic eyepieces evidently completed.

'I hardly like saying it, boss,' Molly remarked, but there are an awful lot of holes in your theory — apart from the fact that it doesn't seem to work.'

'Holes?' Quirke aimed a gloomy look. 'Sit down and tell me where they are — or where they're not.'

He seemed about to rumble in merriment but evidently he was too worried, for his moonlike face became solemn again.

'Well, look at it this way . . . ' Molly smiled her thanks to the guardian constable who drew up a chair for her. 'You're dead set on this web-filter idea over the telescope — '

'Because it is correct. Nothing will ever change my mind about that.'

'But if that be so where did the web go to? The police didn't find anything on the object glass and you know they'd examine the reflector from top to bottom. Neither did we when we examined it later — or rather you did. The web just couldn't vanish after being woven, unless somebody deliberately removed it.'

'Nobody removed it,' Quirke responded. 'And the answer to that is perfectly simple. The spider wove its web, Brunner died because of something he saw which the web *caused*, and after that a wind of hurricane force blew the web to Hades. That was why no traces were left. The wind got up suddenly and became severe:

I've checked on that. The web wouldn't stand a chance up there with a hurricane blowing . . . '

'Oh . . . ' Molly looked rather shame-faced. 'Sorry, A.Q. I'd quite forgotten about the gale.'

'You shouldn't. It's your business to remember . . . ' Quirke broke off and smiled amiably. 'Sorry, my love. I'm a bit edgy at the moment. It's annoying to have everything fit in theoretically and then find it doesn't work.'

'Then let's try another way,' Molly said, feeling she ought to make amends. 'What exactly do you think did happen to Brunner? That he saw something which burned out his optic nerves and destroyed his brain, or part of it?'

'Yes. And if it happened to him it should have happened to me, but it didn't. That's the puzzle! Nor did it affect the rest of you!'

'Maybe the light of Betelgeuse isn't quite the same tonight as it was the other night?'

Quirke smiled sadly. 'You can do better than that, Molly! Stars don't alter their outpourings of radiation from night to night!'

'Perhaps the atmosphere isn't as clear, then? That might cause some special light wave to be blocked!'

'Light waves, m'dear, are all of the same order. The only difference lies in the colour wavelengths. *All* the colours are getting through, so that is not the answer.'

'C'm on, Loony . . . *C'm on!*' It was Joe shuffling across to the reflector and holding out his hand to the busy insect as it dropped from its labours beside the object glass. 'Time you had a meal, young feller — an' there'll be no nasty Dr. Brunner to kick you about or 'ave you destroyed, neither.'

Quirke looked up suddenly, and Molly knew that action intimately. Something had abruptly ignited in the analytical brain.

'A moment, Joe . . . ' Quirke heaved to his feet and went over ponderously to where the janitor stood with the insect swinging from his wrist. 'Did Dr. Brunner hate that insect enough to kick it about?'

Joe sighed. ''E tried many a time to put

his shoe through it, Mr. Quirke. At other times he tried to brain it with a chair. 'ated the sight of poor old Loony, 'e did.'

'And Loony naturally hated the sight of him?'

'S'pose so. Can't tell what a hinsect is thinkin', can you? This one's mighty intelligent, so I s'pose 'e *did* 'ate Dr. Brunner, come to think of it.'

'In that respect,' Quirke said absently, 'Dr. Brunner was almost unique. I never heard of anybody else hating these insects, or even disliking them. They're too fascinating for that. So I wonder what Dr. Brunner's grievance was?'

'If you ask me, Mr. Quirke, Dr. Brunner just 'ated everything as a matter of course! Well, if you're not wantin' Loony any more I'll give 'im 'is food — '

'Yes, do that,' Quirke assented, thinking; then after a moment he looked at Molly. 'No living creature, Molly — and that includes insects and even amoeba — ever forgets ill treatment, and it is the natural wild instinct which demands retaliation somewhere, somehow, some day. The more intelligent the creature the more subtle the revenge. That Loony, a highly developed Martian spider, loathed Brunner is now quite clear. And that would seem to suggest that the insect deliberately murdered Brunner!'

Molly raised her eyebrows. 'Gosh, A.Q., you're flying high now, aren't you? To say that also means the creature had the intelligence to know that, by weaving a fatal web, it could bring about Brunner a destruction!'

'I believe it *did* know it.'

Molly stared blankly, by now completely lost.

'I believe it knew it,' Quirke continued, 'because it had the instinctive power of knowing Brunner's real origin. It knew it could destroy him by light-wave malformation because it had probably used the same method before, in a different way, to wipe out its enemies!'

'Boss, I'm only human and very dense sometimes. This is one of those moments when I completely fail to register!'

'Come back home to the lab, and I'll show you exactly what I mean.'

Quirke turned quickly, all thought of

the observatory apparently gone from his mind. He said nothing during the drive home, and when the laboratory had been reached he went to the bookcase. Then he turned to look at Molly as she settled into a chair.

'You will recall from your interplanetary history that all Martian vegetation and life did not originate on that planet. It was imported from Earth, after Mars was colonized. The early settlers were skilled scientists, and they cultivated quite large forest, jungle, and agricultural areas under their pressurised domes, in order to make themselves self-sufficient from Earth.'

Molly wrinkled her brow. 'But our pet spider — and quite a few other Martian insects and animals — are quite different to anything we have on Earth. We don't have any insects with anything like the rudimentary intelligence possessed by Loony . . . How come?'

'That's easily explained,' Quirke said, running his fingers along a row of reference books. 'The surface of Mars is subjected to considerable background cosmic radiation — far more than gets through on Earth — and that gave rise to a high incidence of mutations, of which Loony is a prime example — Ah, here it is.'

Quirke picked up the volume on *The Mutated Fauna of Mars* and brought it across to where Molly was sitting. Opening the book, he stubbed a plump finger at a long paragraph.

'Read!' he directed. 'Out loud! From that you'll see where I got my basic idea from.'

Molly rested the volume in her bandaged hands and looked at the passage Quirke had indicated. Quirke lighted his briar and listened absorbedly as she read —

''Probably the most unique method ever devised by prodigal Nature is used by the Martian gossamer-spider for slaying its enemies. It first assails its foe in the normal way and by mandible and pincer claws gains the mastery, but does not slay. Instead it weaves its deadly web about the still-living insectile victim and then leaves it. Death comes quickly because through the web the light-waves are warped and twisted incredibly. The hapless insect within the web, viewing its surroundings through this web, sees only a nightmare of distorted, prismatic colours. This affects the unusually sensitive optic nerves of the creatures, rapidly producing blindness and then death by the transmission shock to the brain itself via the optic nerves. It is an established fact, according to the Earth medical experts who have examined Mars-born humans as well as insect and animal life, that all seeing creatures on that planet have hyper-sensitive optic nerves. This is the direct outcome of living on a planet of perpetual twilight, due to Mars' distance from the sun, where sunlight such as we enjoy on Earth is never seen. Over successive generations their optic nerves have become extremely reactive organs'.'

'That's enough,' Quirke said. 'You see now how I worked out my theory?'

'Yes, I see. But it still didn't work, A.Q.!'

'It did on Brunner, but not on me. There's only one answer to that: Brunner was differently constructed to me, or you, or anybody of this Earth. He must at root have been a Martian, and Loony knew it, through that instinctive power which the lower creatures have of knowing their own kind. It knew that Brunner would have the same sensitive optics as the rest of his race. It knew he could be killed that way.'

Molly reflected. 'Brunner was a Teuton, wasn't he?'

'Apparently, yes. Mind you, he could have been born on Earth, but if his original stock was Martian he'd carry a lot of the Martian strains within him.'

'If you're right,' Molly said slowly, 'how are we ever to prove it? Brunner's dead, and his optic nerves are so destroyed you can't tell now whether they were similar to ours or not.'

'True enough.' Quirke dragged at his briar for a moment. 'I do feel, from Brunner's anatomical construction, that he was born of Earth parents, but somewhere there was the Martian strain which gave him the hyper-sensitive optic nerves. That may also account for his eminence as an astronomer. It was well known that he could see further into space than most experts in his line . . . The thing to do,' Quirke finished, 'is have the Bureau of Records trace his history back as far as possible.'

With that he turned quickly to the telephone and contacted the ever-open Bureau of Records in the city centre.

Half an hour passed, Quirke never uttering a word as he sucked at his dead pipe and lost himself in thought. Molly too remained silent. Then as last the 'phone shrilled.

'Quirke here . . . ' He held the instrument and waited.

'Here's the information, Mr. Quirke. Henry Brunner was born of a German father and Austrian mother. The connections on the father's side are all German, but on the mother's side there are distinct English ancestors.'

'Damn!' Quirke swore. 'Anything else?'

'Only Brunner's life record. Began his career as astronomical observer on one of the first space fleets, and also went with the early expeditions to Mars. Was married to Eva Raynor, of Mars, in

Twenty-One Sixty-Six. His intention was to settle with her in the Martian capital city, but a fatal disease brought about Eva's death in Twenty-One Sixty-Nine. Brunner, though medically 'naturalised' to the conditions of Mars, like all other settlers there, returned to Earth and resumed his position as professional astronomer. Then he — '

'I think that's enough, thank you,' Quirke interrupted. 'I'm much obliged to you for the information.'

He rang off and Molly, who had clearly heard the conversation, was still looking puzzled.

'Doesn't get us anywhere even now, does it? Brunner was an Earthman with no Martian characteristics.'

'An Earthman, yes — but with *many* Martian characteristics, m'dear!' Quirke was beaming with delight. 'He was medically naturalised to the Martian conditions, which is very similar to Earth people being inoculated. Yes indeed! Brunner would be very much of a Martian by the time the medical treatment was over, so much so, I fancy, that he even had his character influenced by Martian sentiments. His hatred of gossamer-spiders was one sample of it, perhaps originally engendered by his luckless wife. It seems pretty certain now that Brunner, by medical naturalisation, became so much of a Martian in outlook and physique, that the gossamer-spider in the observatory was led to thinking he *was* one.'

'Which would account for his Martian eyesight?'

'Very easily. Mars, being more distant from the sun, receives only a fraction of the sunlight we do. The Martian geneticists have therefore bred for larger pupils in the eyes of their own people, over successive generations. New settlers, such as Brunner was, would receive special medical treatment to help him adapt. Why, even as far back as World War Two, more than two centuries ago, night-pilots were given drugs which greatly increased their powers of seeing in the dark. How much more, then, would modern drugs produce an effect? We have our answer there, Molly, as to why Brunner was affected and we were not, but the task now is to prove it to that very hide-bound Commissioner of Police.'

'We certainly can't demonstrate with a corpse,' Molly admitted.

'True. There might be another way, though.' Quirke turned again to the telephone and contacted the Commissioner's home. The hour was still not late enough for him to have retired, and after a moment or two his voice came through.

'Oh, it's you, Quirke! Got something definite at the eleventh hour?'

'I have the whole business sorted out, together with the explanation for my not being affected by tonight's experiment at the observatory. It's too long a tale now for me to go into the details; they can come later. My request at the moment is for a condemned Martian prisoner to act as a stand-in for Brunner.'

'To do *what*? What in the world are you talking about?'

Quirke gave a patient little sigh and reflected that the Commissioner of Police could be very dense sometimes.

'On your list of condemned prisoners,

Commissioner, you must have quite a few pure-born Martians, who are awaiting the lethal chamber for some crime or other of which they have been convicted. Select me a Martian who is due for an early fate and find out if he is prepared to take his penalty in a different way to that given by the lethal chamber. I know it isn't constitutional and you'll have to get the prisoner's full sanction — but it's the one way of proving what *did* happen to Brunner.'

The Commissioner gave an indignant snort. 'There's not a cat in hell's chance of your request being granted, Quirke! According to your reckoning, death by that reflector-mirror is protracted and anguishing. In the lethal chamber it's humane and swift. No prisoner would trade a lingering, painful death for a quick one.'

'He doesn't *have* to be told it's a lingering death.'

'What kind of a game are you playing, Quirke? There are laws to protect even criminals! If I can find a volunteer, which I very much doubt, I am compelled to state every fact — and you know it.'

'I know it, yes — and I also know that unless we pull every trick on the board we'll never get that convincing proof we need and an innocent man might be condemned. It's not you who need the proof, Commissioner, but your superiors as well. I'll want them to be present at the demonstration. I do know that by the Constitution you are allowed to ask for a volunteer, so do that and see what happens. If we get no result we'll try something else. Right?'

'Very well,' the Commissioner agreed grudgingly. 'But I don't like it.'

Quirke shrugged and switched off, glancing at Molly.

'It isn't a question of whether he likes it or not, nor is it a matter of how a convicted criminal dies. We must have the proof we need and only a Martian can supply it.'

'And if you get one, and he dies as Brunner did, can you explain all the other parts? The scratches on the mirror, the blow on the head? I know you've cleaned up the prints on the throat but these other factors are still outstanding.'

'They'll fit in of themselves,' Quirke replied. 'You'll see . . . For the moment, light of my life, there's nothing more we can do but hope for a volunteer. That being so we'd better pack it in for tonight and I'll see you at the usual time in the morning.'

★ ★ ★

It was towards eleven the following morning when the Commissioner arrived in Quirke's laboratory. With him was a quiet, middle-aged half-breed — Earth-Martian — dressed in the sombre black of a prisoner condemned by the Inter-planetary High Court. From the look of him he was more of an intellectual than a killer.

'Here's your man, Quirke,' the Commissioner said gruffly. 'His name is Virgil Lanson — Earth mother, Martian father. From the medical reports at the prison his physical structure is mainly Martian and that's what you want, isn't it?'

Quirke nodded, studying the prisoner intently. For his own part Virgil Lanson made no comment: he simply surveyed Quirke's gigantic form and held his counsel.

'You understand what you are called upon to do?' Quirke asked at length, his face grim.

'I gather that I am to sacrifice my life some hours sooner than I would otherwise do. I am prepared to do that because of the financial consideration that is granted to prisoners who volunteer for a suicidal task rather than meet their end in the lethal chamber. 'It so happens,' Lanson explained, 'that I have a wife and two children in desperate straits and the State compensation — which my being a volunteer will permit them to receive — may set them on the road to re-establishing themselves.'

Quirke nodded. For the moment he had overlooked that the State granted any prisoner a large tax-free lump sum to be delegated to whomsoever he or she chose, in the event of sentence not being carried out according to law.

'Those details are correct, Commissioner?' Quirke asked.

'Quite! I've made the necessary arrangements. Virgil Lanson was scheduled to die at four this afternoon. His volunteering actually means a few hours longer life since I suppose your test will be made tonight?'

'At eight o'clock, weather permitting,' Quirke responded. 'The Weather Bureau expects the fine spell to continue so there should be no trouble about that . . . Now, Lanson, you have been told everything and you know that you will meet death in a painful, even somewhat lingering, form?'

'As I understand it from the Commissioner you intend to use me as guinea-pig to a gossamer-spider. I am prepared for that — chiefly because I am gambling on the thousand-to-one chance that I might escape. The law states that if a volunteer should survive a suicidal experiment he is entitled to his freedom.'

'In this instance, my friend, I do not see any chance of that,' Quirke said quietly; then he turned back to the

216

Commissioner. 'Tonight, then, Commissioner, and if you wish to bring your superiors with you to the observatory it will be quite all right to me.'

'No necessity for that, Quirke. I'm still in charge of the Brunner case and if I'm satisfied with the solution they will have to be, too.'

With that the Commissioner turned aside, jerked his head briefly to the condemned man, then followed him to the door. Quirke watched them through the televisor screen as they departed, and then compressed his lips. Molly, who had been a silent witness of the interview, looked at him in some reproach.

'I hate to say it, A.Q., but you have a ruthless streak which I never suspected. You are calmly prepared to send that poor devil to his death.'

'Since that is to be his fate anyhow he might as well die usefully, Molly. In my business I cannot afford to have sentiments in regard to individuals, because if I do somebody quite innocent will get hurt. Scientific proof always demands cruel sacrifices — even of life itself. The one fact remains — that proof we have *got to have*!'

There was nothing more to be said. Quirke had made his decision and thereby revealed to the vaguely discomfited Molly that he could be just as tough as benign when the circumstances demanded it. He did not even refer to the matter again during the day but spent the time bringing his notes on the case up to date in readiness for handing over to the authorities with his expenses account when the job was done. Molly, unable to write or type, helped as best she could by reading out the various references he required.

★ ★ ★

So at last eight o'clock arrived, and when Molly and Quirke arrived within the observatory they found the Commissioner already present, together with Virgil Lanson, the constable on duty, and the police surgeon whose duty it would be to pronounce whether or not the condemned man was dead. That he was paying his penalty in a different way from that prescribed by law made no difference to the law in regard to a surgeon certifying that life was extinct.

'Far as I'm concerned,' the Commissioner said, 'all the legal formalities in regard to this business are complete. The job is now up to you.'

Quirke nodded and turned to the control board, closing the switch that set the two hemispheres of roof rolling aside.

Quirke's next move was to ascend laboriously to the parapet and examine the reflector's object glass. The web spun by Loony the night before was still there since the closed roof had prevented any destruction from the strong wind, if indeed anything short of a full-blown gale could destroy that intricate mesh.

Satisfied so far, Quirke returned to the floor of the laboratory and made the necessary calculations for the reflector's position. There were but few adjustments to make to sight it directly upon Betelgeuse; then he set the electric motor in action and the great instrument began to turn slowly.

Virgil Lanson licked his lips, his only sign of emotion, as Quirke pulled aside the silken velvet covering the mirror — then he came slowly across the laboratory and looked steadily at the silent half-breed.

'This is the moment, my friend,' he said quietly.

Virgil Lanson did not comment and he ignored the hand that Quirke held out to him. Quirke gave a shrug and then nodded to the girder holding the observation chair.

'Kindly sit in that, Lanson.'

The Earth-Martian went across the observatory and obeyed instructions to the letter.

'On the arms of that chair you'll find buttons,' Quirke continued. 'When I say 'Go!' press the third button on the right arm. You understand?'

Virgil Lanson nodded slowly, staring straight in front of him, his jaw set tightly.

'After which,' Quirke murmured to the Commissioner, 'watch for yourself what happens. Imagine that Lanson there is Brunner and you'll have a demonstration of what happened on that fatal night.'

The Commissioner settled himself to watch, but Molly still kept turned away. Inwardly she wished she had cried off from being present at this demonstration, but after all, as Quirke's secretary she had to be present.

'Go!' Quirke ordered suddenly.

Immediately Lanson pressed the third button, and that caused the object glass of the huge reflector to become unmasked. Involuntarily the half-breed looked down into the swirling sea of colours below him. It was as though he were hypnotised for a second or two, then suddenly he gave a scream and clapped both hands to his eyes, his fingers spread out across his forehead. He had not the strength to move. He lurched forward in the chair, gasping with pain, and suddenly fell on to the mirror itself. There he remained, writhing, his hands still clapped over his eyes.

'Get him away from there!' the Commissioner panted. 'I can't stand any more of this!'

The constable, who assumed the order

was meant for him, hurried forward and caught at the screaming prisoner's jacket collar, dragging him clear of the mirror and on to the observatory floor. Immediately the surgeon advanced and made a quick examination of the groaning man.

'How is he?' Quirke came lumbering up.

'Far from dead, anyhow. His heart is racing from shock but it will settle down.'

'What about his eyes?'

This the surgeon found a difficult task. For a long time Lanson could not be persuaded to lower his hands. When at last he did so there appeared to be nothing unusual about his eyes, except for the fact that they were bloodshot and watering.

'Can you see, Lanson?' the surgeon demanded, and the man nodded slowly, his face drawn.

'Yes — I can see, but I feel as though pins and needles are behind my eyes.'

'That will go,' Quirke said, straightening up. 'Condemned prisoner though you may have been, my friend — for you are now a free man, having cheated death

— you are a man of exceptional courage. You showed us all we needed to know but saved yourself, unwittingly perhaps, by covering your eyes almost instantly with your hands. And why did you do that? Because you had been told beforehand what to expect. That right?'

'That's right,' Lanson assented, calming. 'The moment I felt those colours tearing into my eyes and brain I blotted them out with my hands and — I suppose that saved my life?'

'Exactly!' Quirke was beaming genially. 'I rather thought that being forewarned you'd save yourself and give us our proof as well. You are prepared to state that had you continued to gaze at those colours being radiated from Betelgeuse you would have died?'

'I'm convinced of it! They didn't look like colours to me — they were vibrations! Lethal vibrations driving into my brain and burning out my sight.'

'Which,' Quirke mused, 'shows how Martian eyes see colour vibration differently from us. Is that part clear enough to you, Commissioner?

The Commissioner was not looking too pleased. 'I can see that Martian optic nerves, which Brunner also possessed through medical naturalisation, are hyper-sensitive to the colour vihrations radiated by the stars — '

'And by ruddy Betelgeuse in particular!' Quirke held up a finger. 'Red colour, even to Earth beings, is a difficult wavelength to tolerate. To hypersensitive optics it is evidently completely lethal.'

'Evidently. Yes, Quirke, I can see all that — but I can't think why Brunner hadn't the sense to cover his eyes as Lanson did!'

'The reason for that, I think, relies on the simple fact that he was not expecting what he saw. He believed he would see the normal Betelgeuse. Instead he got the filtered colour-wavelengths caused by Loony's web. What more natural than that he should stare and stare in wonder — until suddenly the wavelengths had effect and blasted at him with overwhelming force. He was probably blinded and, tormented with pain, he tumbled out of his chair and staggered across the mirror — hence the scratches from his shoes as he moved. They follow a lurching, zig-zag trace if you care to study them closely . . .

'And then,' Quirke finished, spreading his hands, 'he collided with the telescope's manual arm, which is the nearest low down solid object to the point where those scratches end. It is obvious from the force with which he hit it that he was moving fast and could not see where he was going. And finally, clutching frantically at his throat, as one does when life is ebbing, he crashed to the floor, his dying scream reaching the ears of the janitor.'

The Commissioner was silent for a long moment. 'The way you tell it, Quirke, it all seems so logical.'

'Never mind about the way *I* tell it, man. Have your men measure up the distance from scratches on the mirror to the manual arm. Have our surgeon friend here look again at that blow on Brunner's head — Do anything you like, but it all adds up to the same thing. If you, or your superiors, are still then unsatisfied, have the ex-prisoner examined. Make tests of his eyes and determine their hypersensitivity to filtered red wavelength . . . You've got your answer, Commissioner, and I've nothing more to add. If you'll send round to my place tomorrow — or late tonight — you can have my dossier on the whole case. You'll find everything drops right into place.'

The Commissioner relaxed and gave a rueful smile. 'Knowing you, Quirke, I'm taking your word for all this. It's one of those complex scientific mysteries which are part of our day and age and which only men like you can solve.'

'And which only men like this can *prove*,' Quirke added, clapping the now half-smiling Lanson on the shoulder. 'And, Commissioner, I imagine the State's face will be somewhat red! They have failed to carry out the death sentence, have given away thousands of pounds, and are compelled to let their man go free.'

'It's justice anyway,' Lanson said, shrugging. 'I was wrongfully accused of murder. Circumstantial evidence which I couldn't break down, so that I'm now free is only just.'

'If you get into a tangle like that again

call me.' Quirke grinned. 'The Commissioner will just love that!'

The Commissioner did not seem to hear. 'If I arrest anybody,' he said slowly, 'it ought to be Joe for having that spider. I can hardly arrest a spider, can I?'

'You can,' Quirke replied solemnly, 'but you'd look mighty silly doing it!

The observatory began to quiver. Molly raised one eyebrow, and the Commissioner waited with empurpled face for the merriment from the man-mountain to subside.

THE END

We do hope that you have enjoyed reading this large print book.

Did you know that all of our titles are available for purchase?

We publish a wide range of high quality large print books including:
Romances, Mysteries, Classics
General Fiction
Non Fiction and Westerns

Special interest titles available in large print are:
The Little Oxford Dictionary
Music Book, Song Book
Hymn Book, Service Book

Also available from us courtesy of Oxford University Press:
Young Readers' Dictionary
(large print edition)
Young Readers' Thesaurus
(large print edition)

For further information or a free brochure, please contact us at:
Ulverscroft Large Print Books Ltd.,
The Green, Bradgate Road, Anstey,
Leicester, LE7 7FU, England.
Tel: (00 44) **0116 236 4325**
Fax: (00 44) **0116 234 0205**

Other titles in the
Linford Mystery Library:

A TIME FOR MURDER

John Glasby

Carlos Galecci, a top man in organized crime, has been murdered — and the manner of his death is extraordinary . . . He'd last been seen the previous night, entering his private vault, to which only he knew the combination. When he fails to emerge by the next morning, his staff have the metal door cut open — to discover Galecci dead with a knife in his back. Private detective Johnny Merak is hired to find the murderer and discover how the impossible crime was committed — but is soon under threat of death himself . . .

THE MASTER MUST DIE

John Russell Fearn

Gyron de London, a powerful industrialist of the year 2190, receives a letter warning him of his doom on the 30th March, three weeks hence. Despite his precautions — being sealed in a guarded, radiation-proof cube — he dies on the specified day, as forecast! When scientific investigator Adam Quirke is called to investigate, he discovers that de London had been the victim of a highly scientific murder — but who was the murderer, and how was this apparently impossible crime committed?

DR. MORELLE AND THE DRUMMER GIRL

Ernest Dudley

'Dear Mr. Drummer. Your daughter is safe . . . If you want her back alive it is going to cost you money . . . Don't call the police . . . You are under observation, so don't try any tricks.' A note is left in the girl's flat by her kidnapper. Her father, Harvey Drummer, turns to Dr. Morelle and Miss Frayle to help him secure his daughter's release. The case proves to be one of the most baffling and hazardous of the Doctor's career!

MONTENEGRIN GOLD

Brian Ball

Discovering his late father's war diaries, Charles Copley learns that he had been involved in counter-intelligence. When Charles is approached by an organisation trying to buy the diaries, he refuses. But he is viciously attacked — and then his son is murdered . . . Seeking revenge, he is joined by Maria Wright, daughter of his father's wartime friend. They are led on a journey to the mountains of Montenegro — and thirty years back in time in search of a lost treasure.

MOON BASE

E. C. Tubb

On the surface of the Moon the 'cold war' continues: world powers watch each other and wait . . . After a series of mysterious events, Britain's Moon Base personnel are visited by a Royal Commission. Among them is Felix Larsen, there to secretly probe the possibility of espionage. But he faces many inexplicable incidents . . . What are the strange messages emanating from the Base? Where are they from? And what is the fantastic thing that has been conceived in the research department?

DEAD FOR DANGER

Lorette Foley

When a young Dublin woman is mugged and afterwards stabbed, the police look in vain for the attacker. But 49 Organ Place, the seedy apartment house where she lived, holds the secret which links her fate with that of a desperate and hunted man ... Detective Inspector Moss Coen is baffled by the discovery of another body. But when all the tenants suffer a final, devastating and deadly attack, the Inspector must go all out to find a merciless killer.